COURAGE

CHELSI ARNOLD

Courage

Bienvenue Press, LLC
Youngsville, LA 70592
http://www.bienvenuepress.com

Formatting: Charms Formatting

In honor of the courageous men and women who have given the ultimate sacrifice for our country. You will never be forgotten.

America will never be destroyed from the outside. If we falter and lose our freedoms, it will be because we destroyed ourselves.

- Abraham Lincoln

Chapter 1

"I AM SO SORRY."

A small white cloud hovered in front of my face as I released another breath. My gaze drifted over the layer of snow blanketing a pair of angel wings. The tips of the wings brushed the ground, patiently waiting for a strong gust of wind to lift them up into the air.

I reached out and gently ran a finger over a grey feather. I expected to feel warmth and softness, but instead, cold seeped from the hard slab. Sighing, I looked down at the grey heart embedded within the wings.

A large lump began forcing its way down my throat.

Angelette…

Below her intricately carved name, Angelette's bright smile brought warmth and life to the concrete. Her green eyes shined up at me.

Feeling strength from her gaze, I took a deep breath as I crouched down and gently placed flowers on the snow-covered ground.

"It's been two months…"

The lump shoved its way farther down my throat, making it difficult to breathe.

Come on, Greer, get it together.

Swallowing, I took another breath. "It's been two months, and not a day goes by that I don't miss you."

A small ray of sunlight peeked through the dark clouds,

causing a smile to pop onto my frozen face. I tilted my head toward the light and saw a flash of blue streak overhead. Shifting my gaze to a nearby tree, I watched as a small blue jay landed on one of the limbs.

"Hello, Angelette." Rubbing my hands together, I stood. "I'm meeting with the girls in a few hours. It's our last hoorah before judgement."

Anger drifted through me.

Clenching my teeth, I patted the top of a wing. "Senior says this should be the end…" I glanced back at Angelette's picture and smiled. "I couldn't leave without telling you goodbye."

Crunching footsteps sounded behind me. My muscles tensed as I spun around.

A petite woman with grey curls slowly walked down the path. She kept her head down, staring at the road as she avoided ice patches. I started to turn back around when she suddenly looked up.

I sucked in a breath.

Green eyes I thought I'd never see again stared directly at me.

My heartbeat continued to accelerate the longer I gaped at the green eyes. Her gaze swept over my body and then darted down to the flowers lying on the ground. I watched as her lips formed a thin line.

"Get away from my daughter."

Unable to move, I stood there as if my feet had been cemented to the ground. Her lips began to pinch together when I continued to gawk. I knew I needed to say something, but my mind couldn't get past the green eyes.

Angelette's eyes.

The longer I stared, the more I noticed a difference between the green eyes that haunted my dreams and the ones right in front of me. Angelette's eyes had always been filled with light and joy, while this woman's gaze held only sorrow and pain.

Angelette's mom took a step toward me, her closed fists shaking. "I said. Get. Away. From. My. Daughter."

Regaining my senses, I took a hesitant step away from the stone wings. "Ma'am, I was a friend of your daughter's." My voice cracked, and I had to take a painful swallow.

She narrowed her eyes. "I know who you are. You killed my daughter."

The sting in her tone cut deeper than the frigid December air. I opened my mouth, but nothing came out.

How did she know me?

The events at Damascus had been broadcasted nonstop since the attack, but no one knew the identities of those involved. Not even my parents.

Seeing my wrinkled forehead, Angelette's mom sneered. "My Angelette would talk about you and the others. She looked up to you, and *you* got her killed."

Her words sucked the air from my constricted lungs. I closed my eyes and tried to breathe past the large lump clogging my throat. Images of Angelette's bright, excited face flashed behind my eyelids.

The winter wind felt like the sting of flying dust and debris. Smoke filled my nose as a single fired shot rang in my ears.

Round green eyes stared deeply into mine. Horror slowly spread across Angelette's face as blood spurted from her neck. Seconds felt more like years as the life drained from her eyes.

Gasping, my eyes snapped open. I could see Angelette's mother's mouth opening and closing, but the insults she hurled failed to penetrate my imprisoning nightmare.

I looked away from Angelette's mom and down to my shaking hands. Blood stained my white gloves.

Breathe, Greer.

It took several rapid heartbeats for the crimson liquid to slowly transform back into white fabric. Inhaling deeply, I opened and closed my hands until my heart rate slowed.

"You all deserve to be locked up."

At that, my head snapped up. The need to defend my sisters had my mouth parting, but when I noticed the tears pooling in her green eyes, my retort died.

Unlike some people in this country, I could see she didn't mean what she said. My fingers unclenched as I stared at the grieving mother.

"She shouldn't have been there." Tears streaked down her face. "Your job was to protect my baby and you failed." A broken sob burst from her lips. "You didn't save my baby girl…my Angel."

Tears pricked at my eyes as I took a small step forward. "Ma'am, I'm…"

Her narrowed gaze prevented the rest of my words from coming out. My skin felt scorched from where her eyes burned me.

"Leave."

I looked back at Angelette's smiling face. I barely glimpsed her joyous expression before her mother stepped in front of me. Her body lined up perfectly with the concrete wings, making her look like an avenging angel.

"I don't want Angelette to have anything to do with the military or the CIA." She took another step closer to me and placed her hands on her hips. "And I especially don't want her to have anything to do with you."

I lost the battle with my tears. I felt a few glide down my cheek as they left behind a frozen trail.

"I said leave!" Angelette's mom wailed.

The grief became too much for her petite frame to hold any longer. Her shoulders slumped as her head fell to her chest. The lump in my throat threatened to strangle me as she wrapped a protective arm around her stomach.

"I'm so sorry," I whispered.

Her tortured sobs filled my ears as I backed away. Using the back of my hand, I wiped the tears from my face. The snow crunched under my feet as I shuffled past Angelette's mom. I tried to concentrate on the soft winter breeze and my loud footsteps, but nothing could muffle the broken sobs coming from her lips.

A dark shadow fell over me. Glancing up, I watched as a large cloud pushed away the last remaining ray of sunlight. Sighing, I stuffed my hands deep into my pockets and trudged out of the cemetery.

"We could use your light now more than ever, Angelette," I whispered.

As if it agreed with my statement, the alarm on my watch began beeping.

A cold chill crept down my spine.

I touched the small wing earring I had gotten pierced in my cartilage. I glanced once more at the dark sky, hoping for just a small glimpse of sunshine. When the clouds remained, I released my pent-up breath and sadly shook my head.

"Almost judgement time…"

Chapter 2

THE WINTER WIND STRENGTHENED ITS BITTER ASSAULT against my exposed skin just as the small red building came into sight. Muffled chanting floated in with the frigid gusts of air, and I tensed.

For a heartbeat, my stride faltered as I scanned the area. People bundled up in their winter clothes rushed in and out of stores, their hands full with shopping bags. Tall buildings decorated with twinkling lights and wreaths stood proudly along the street.

Taking a deep breath, I unclenched my fists and walked briskly toward the diner. A rush of warm air thawed my frozen cheeks as I stomped the snow from my shoes. Breathing in the enticing aroma of burgers and fries, I looked over the occupants of the room.

A group of young men huddled around the bar, their unwavering gazes fixed on the television screen. My lips curved up into an amused grin when they all let out disappointed groans. Behind the moaning Redskins fans, a family of four sat in a small booth near the corner. I struggled to keep from laughing as the mother frantically shoved napkins at the two little girls who had cheese dripping off their chins and onto their pink dresses. Smiling, I shifted my attention from the two messy eaters to the dirty windowpane above them. Through the smudges, I could just make out a group of war protestors with their signs.

Clueless dumb bunnies.

Rolling my eyes, I stepped further into the diner and shrugged out of my coat. A young waitress with a bouncy blonde ponytail smiled warmly at me.

"How many?"

I smiled back as my gaze drifted over the area again. "I'm actually meeting—"

"I hope it snows harder," a loud, familiar voice grumbled, effectively cutting me off.

Fighting the urge to laugh at Amerie's bluntness, I turned toward the waitress. "Never mind, I found them."

I eased past the young girl and rounded the corner. My smile grew when my sisters came into view. Sitting around a small table at the back of the diner, Dee propped her head up with her hand while Emersyn and Amerie sat next to one another with bright, round eyes. Emersyn turned toward Amerie and began talking with her hands, causing my cheek muscles to ache.

Shaking my head, I watched Dee roll her eyes and glance down at her watch. Unable to hold it in, a small chuckle escaped my lips as I walked toward the empty seat next to her.

Dee looked up and beamed at me. "Hey, Kid. You made it."

I wriggled my eyebrows at her. "Long time, no see." My gaze drifted to her ear, where she wore a wing earring identical to mine.

The lump threatened to appear again, but Amerie's voice shoved it away. "About time you show up."

Sitting down, I smirked at Amerie. My eyes narrowed when I noticed she sported a new piercing. I lifted my eyebrows and stared pointedly at the small stud in her nose. "We leave you alone for two weeks…"

Amerie touched the stud with the tip of her finger. "Angelette and I had a bet…I lost." She cleared her throat as a somber glint entered her eyes.

Next to me, Dee touched the wing charm on her earring. Across the table, Emersyn glanced down at her wrist where black angel wings were inked on her skin. A sad smile flitted onto my lips as I recalled the taunting and teasing Amerie had given Dee and me for not getting the tattoo on our wrists like her and Emersyn.

The familiar lump found its way back to my throat as a cloud of grief descended upon our little table.

Trying to lighten the mood, I resorted to my secret weapon: sarcasm. "Why didn't you get it done when we were all at Mike's? Scared you'd cry in front of us when that needle pierced your skin?"

Amerie rolled her eyes. "I laughed while I got the tattoo Sheba and you were too scared to get."

Dee shrugged. "I don't have a problem with needles…it's my granny that scares me." She glanced at all of us and shuddered. "She'd tan my hide if I came home with a tattoo."

Our soft laughter pushed away the rest of the lingering melancholy. Amerie touched the stud again before meeting my gaze. "I thought about getting it done at Mike's, but the bet clearly stated I had to get it done at a certain place in Colorado."

"Losing bets sucks, don't it?" I leaned back in my seat and crossed my arms. "That's how I got stuck with your pain-in-the-ass self." A smile curved my lips as I recalled meeting Amerie for the first time and the bet we had made on the plane.

Best thing that ever happened to me.

Out of the corner of my eye, the young waitress strolled toward our table. Our laughter and teasing stopped as she pulled out her notepad and beamed down at us. "Is everyone ready to order?"

Emersyn handed over our menus with a smile. "We just want a large order of loaded fries and five Coronas."

The waitress looked over each of us, silently counting. "I can bring out the four beers now, but I have to wait until your friend gets here."

A soft sigh came from Emersyn. She broke eye contact with the waitress and bit down on her lower lip.

I turned toward the girl. "Can you just bring it out?"

She opened her mouth, clearly getting ready to recite the rules to us, but I gently cut her off. "We're not going to drink it. You don't even have to pop the top. It's just our friend…" The lump rushed forward, forcing me to pause and take a swallow. "She's not going to be joining us," I whispered.

The waitress followed my eyes to the empty chair at the front of our table. I watched as understanding slowly seeped into her features.

She gave a small nod. "I'll have that right out."

I watched her leave and then turned back toward my sisters. Emersyn fidgeted with her watch while Amerie stared at her glass of water.

Next to me, Dee shifted in her seat. "That was nice of her."

I nodded. "Guess there are still some good people left in this world after all."

A few minutes passed and the waitress returned with our order. She placed Angelette's beer in front of her chair. "This one is on the house."

Hold it together, Greer.

Choking down the lump, I nodded. "Thank you."

Amerie waited until the waitress left before she raised her bottle in the air. "Here's to you, Angelette." She patted the table in front of the empty chair. "Hope you enjoy your first beer."

We raised our drinks, and each took a sip.

Dee glanced at the lone bottle of Corona. "I can't believe she'd never had a drink before."

Amerie nodded. "I had plans to do a lot of corrupting."

I snickered. "Plans? You had already started corrupting her."

Amerie turned round, innocent eyes on me. "I did no such thing."

I arched an eyebrow while Emersyn and Dee each attempted to smother their laughs. "Oh, so someone else got her hooked on gambling?"

Amerie waved a finger at me. "Now wait a second." The muscles around her mouth twitched as they struggled to keep from tipping up. "Playing cards has nothing to do with corrupting people."

I shook my head and shoved a cheesy fry in my mouth. "Whatever you say, Legacy."

A cold breeze rushed in as someone walked out the back door next to our table. Chanting from the protestors drifted over us.

Amerie turned her head and scowled at the door. I felt my lips tip up.

In three…two…one…

"Idiot hippies."

Chuckling, I shook my head at Amerie.

I had missed this.

The two-week furlough with my family had been great, but despite my parents' efforts to support me through the craziness of the past two months, they just didn't understand.

No one did.

Only my sisters, who had lived the same nightmare, knew

the feelings that plagued me. They were the only ones who understood.

Amerie stuffed a large fry in her mouth and glowered. "If they saw how bad things were over there, they'd be singing a different tune."

Frowning, I glanced out a window at the back of the crowd. "I doubt that."

Emersyn nodded. "To them, fighting doesn't solve anything; it only makes things worse."

Amerie grabbed another fry and sighed. "Yeah, well, we know better. We've been in Damascus…sitting around doing nothing only allowed their numbers to grow. And it made our job that much harder." She looked out the window and shook her head. "I'd much rather fight them over there than on my home soil."

I grabbed my Corona and tipped it back. My gaze shifted away from the crowd to the TV hanging on the wall.

Dee followed my line of sight and sighed. "What do you think the verdict's going to be?"

My stomach knotted as I watched the reporter talk about the infamous email scandal that led to the Damascus attack.

"Does it matter?" Emersyn asked softly. Her brown eyes moved to the TV where the news anchors talked about the role the four anonymous female SEALs had in the attack. "They're not going to prosecute the former president, vice president, secretary of state, and top CIA officials."

I frowned. They should all be locked behind bars.

A middle-aged man in a dark suit stood in front of the White House. "It has been two weeks since the controversial emergency inauguration of the forty-seventh President of the United States, George Macleod." The man glanced at the protestors before turning back to the camera. "As you can see, many are not happy with the historic December inauguration." The camera zoomed in on the man's face. "The question remains how the Damascus investigation will affect President Carlisle's legacy."

Shaking my head, I turned away from the screen. "Her legacy is nothing but corruption and lies."

Amerie glanced at the TV and then back at me. "As long as we get back to work soon, I don't care what happens to them." She shrugged. "They already lost their jobs…can't get much worse for them."

"Well, we did nothing wrong," Dee grumbled, crossing her arms and glaring at the screen. "We shouldn't be put on suspension just because they needed our testimonies for the investigation."

I looked down at my shoulder, remembering my injury. "Yeah, we're all healed and ready to fight." I looked back up at the screen and watched clips of soldiers fighting in Syria and Russia. "America needs all the willing and able bodies she can get."

Amerie snorted. "Yeah, 'cause we all know those snowflakes aren't going to step up to the plate." She tipped back the rest of her beer and stood. Smirking, her green eyes held a fierce glint. "Let's go get our jobs back."

Chapter 3

"N<small>OT MY PRESIDENT</small>! N<small>OT MY PRESIDENT</small>!"

"Hate will not prevail!"

"Bring home the troops!"

"Hate will not prevail!"

"Not my president!"

Clenching my teeth, I pushed and weaved through the crowd of protestors. Grunts and mumbled complaints trailed behind me. I tilted my head back to see Amerie elbowing her way through.

She caught my smirk and shrugged. "What?" She glared at a screeching woman brandishing a homemade sign before meeting my gaze again. "This deplorable has an important meeting to get to."

Shaking my head, I reached the edge of the crowd and pushed through to a clear space on the sidewalk. Free from the sea of bodies, I took a moment to admire the grand white pillars and the American flag proudly waving in the air.

Emersyn stopped next to me. "Not how I imagined seeing the White House for the first time." She tilted her head back and frowned at the protestors who wrapped around the president's estate. "We Americans can lose our freedom only one way…" Her sad eyes drifted over the crowd and she sighed softly. "By destroying ourselves."

Goosebumps chilled my skin.

Before I could comment on Emersyn's ominous words,

Amerie and Dee plowed past the protestors. Amerie's face scrunched up into a grimace as she wiped her arms off.

She turned toward the crowd. "He is your president! He is your—"

I elbowed her hard.

"Oomph." Pivoting around, she glared at me. "What was that for?"

Ignoring her tone, I began walking down the street. "You're going to get us jumped."

Amerie scoffed. "Like we couldn't take those snowflakes."

I glanced over my shoulder. "I think we are under enough scrutiny as it is…" I gave her a pointed look. "They just need one excuse to keep us from work."

Dee nodded. "They ain't worth it."

Amerie grumbled under her breath but didn't argue.

The snow crunched under our feet as we walked. I inhaled deeply and caught the scent of strong spices and fried food. From the corner of my eye, I noticed a line of food trucks a block away from the growing crowd.

I chuckled. That was a good way to make some money.

Amerie walked up next to me and tilted her head toward a white truck at the end of the line. "I'm thinking we stop there after the hearing."

My steps faltered as I gaped at her. "We just ate."

She placed a hand on her hip and stuck out her lower lip. "I'm always starving after these things."

Laughing, I just shook my head and began walking again.

Dee turned toward the food truck and grimaced. "That looks shady. I ain't eating something off that thing."

Amerie and Dee started arguing over post-hearing dinner plans as we continued down the sidewalk. I glanced up at a street sign and then turned down a vacant alleyway. Trash lay scattered across the ground and graffiti marked the sides of the brick buildings.

Dee scrunched up her nose. "Well, this is inviting." She stepped over a broken glass bottle and huffed. "I doubt Marilyn Monroe appreciated having to sneak through this muck."

Emersyn snickered. "This wasn't even here in the sixties." She waved a hand around the grimy alleyway. "These underground entrances and exit tunnels were added a few years ago as a safety precaution against terrorist attacks." Stepping around a foul smelling, wadded-up blanket, she grimaced. "They purposefully trashed this area of D.C. for added concealment."

I glanced back. "How do you know that?"

Emersyn avoided my gaze as she shrugged. "I might have done some research during our furlough."

Dee shook her head. "Of course you did."

Echoes of our heels clacking across the pavement followed us down the alleyway. A man half hidden in the shadows stepped out as we reached the back wall. His wrinkled clothes and facial scruff suggested he had spent several nights in this alley, but I knew better. The way his eyes tracked over us as we stood in front of his broad, imposing frame told me everything I needed to know about this "homeless" man.

I grabbed the lanyard wrapped around my neck and pulled out my clearance pass. The man wordlessly scanned our IDs and then clicked a button on the black remote hooked to his belt loop.

He smiled at us. "Welcome to the White House."

I surveyed the area, but didn't notice any signs of an entrance. I was about to ask where we were supposed to go when the ground around us slowly began to ease down.

At first, I thought I was experiencing my first earthquake, until I noticed the man's smirk. I slammed my mouth shut, causing him to chuckle.

Humor flashed in his brown eyes. "Never gets old."

Emersyn leaned over the edge and glanced down. "It's like an elevator."

A loud click sounded around us, and I glanced up to see we had traveled down about the height of a semi-truck. The man pointed to another man dressed in a black suit. "He'll take you the rest of the way down the tunnel."

Nodding, I stepped off the pavement elevator onto cold concrete. Next to me, Amerie mumbled something under her breath. My lips tipped up as I took in the concrete tomb surrounding us.

I nudged her with my shoulder. "At least it's not dirt and wood beams above us."

Amerie glared at me. "One of these days, *we will* be back in the air…" she whispered.

I had to bite down on my lip to keep from laughing. The man in the suit stepped forward and smiled warmly at us.

"Welcome, ladies." Seeing we had all stepped off the elevator, he began walking down the dimly lit tunnel. "If you would, please follow me."

The cold winter chill seeped through the concrete walls. I shoved my hands deep into my coat pockets and watched as my breath became a small white cloud. From the corner of my eye, I saw Amerie scowl at the ceiling.

If only I had some gravel to toss in the air…

A smug grin curved my lips as I recalled the look on Amerie's face when she thought the tunnel in Damascus had collapsed. Feeling my stare, she turned her head toward me and narrowed her eyes.

"Don't even think about it," she mouthed.

I chuckled, causing Dee to glance over. She looked between Amerie and me and smirked.

A current of heat drifted over my skin just as the ground began to gradually slope up. Instead of following the tunnel, the man curved to the left and walked into a heated room. I stepped into the small space and glanced around.

Cinnamon filled my nose as I walked onto thick tan carpet. Green and red wreaths hung from the cream walls and a small Christmas tree occupied the center of the room.

Following Amerie, I headed toward the makeshift coat rack that claimed nearly a whole wall. Breathing in the sweet cinnamon, I shrugged out of my coat and hung it next to Emersyn's.

The man waited patiently by the tree until we had taken off all of our winter gear. I placed my scarf on top of my coat and met his gaze.

"Ready?" he asked.

I nodded, and he ushered us out of the room and down a hallway. Christmas trees stood guard at every other door. Their twinkling lights danced across the marble floors, providing a mesmerizing show for our entourage. I could feel my inner child jumping inside of me, begging me to tour the rest of the light show.

Beth would love this. I smiled as I imagined her carrot curls bouncing around her head as she tried to take in everything all at once.

The man rounded a corner and then stopped by an oak door and held it open for us. "Good luck," he whispered just as I walked past him.

My stomach tightened, but I managed a small smile. "Thanks."

Plush leather chairs and long oak tables filled the auditorium style room. At the front, a judge-like bench loomed over us. I quickly scanned the nameplates sitting on the massive bench before I turned my attention to the smaller tables.

"Lucky us," Amerie grumbled under her breath. "We get a front row seat."

A surge of adrenaline shot through my veins as a horde of butterflies began twisting and swirling inside of me. Looking down, I found my nameplate placed at the end of our table, directly in front of the bench where Attorney General Franklin would be sitting.

Acting more comfortable than I felt, I eased down into the soft leather chair. I ran my hands over the smooth armrests as I eyed the small microphone in front of me.

Judgment time.

Tingles pricked along the back of my neck, causing me to sit up straighter. Turning my head to the side, I met a pair of glaring beady eyes. My eyes narrowed slightly as I held Chief's gaze. The vein near his temple started to throb and he quickly averted his eyes.

"I can't believe *he* got a medal," Amerie grumbled.

I felt my lips curve up into a humorless smirk. "Well, he did get us that overhead watch with ISR…"

Amerie crossed her arms and scoffed while my mind drifted back to the first time I met Senior. His words from the Physical Screening Test flashed through my mind.

"Senior warned us," I mumbled.

Amerie's brow furrowed. "What?"

I turned toward her and deepened my voice into my best Senior impersonation, "If your intention of becoming a SEAL is to win medals and have your name broadcasted as a hero, you need to get out. This isn't for the fame and glory."

Amerie's lips tipped up as she chuckled. "Pretty sure he made those girls cry."

My smirk grew as I recalled the way Senior had marched

toward us that first day and peered down at our group with a disapproving scowl. Even now, I could still feel my determination to prove to him and everyone else I had what it took to become a SEAL.

I glanced over the filling courtroom and let that same determination surge through me.

I am a fighter.

From the corner of my eye, I noticed four bulky men in suits. I made eye contact with one before my gaze wandered over to former Madam President Carlisle. I schooled my expression into a blank mask as anger filled me.

"I'm so glad she's out of office," Emersyn whispered.

As if she heard Emersyn, President Carlisle glanced at our small group. Her eyes narrowed, but she plastered a sinister smile on her face. Always the politician.

She glanced away and took a seat in front of Chief. Resisting the urge to glare at the two of them, I turned my attention back to the bench and took a deep breath. The salty scent of the ocean drifted over me. I felt myself breathing in the welcoming aroma as a large shadow loomed over the table.

"Hey, Pops." Amerie turned around and beamed at Senior.

He shook his head at the nickname Amerie used off the field. Even though Senior acted insulted by the name, his eyes always softened at the endearment. We were his girls.

A rare grin lifted Senior's lips. "Almost there. You'll all be back to work soon." His gaze shifted to the opposite side of the room where President Carlisle sat. His eyes narrowed slightly before moving back toward us. "We'll get you back where you're needed after this."

Senior's tone caused an uneasy feeling to settle in my stomach.

Frowning, I noticed the dark shadows under his eyes and the extra grey streaks in his hair. I didn't know any of the specifics about the war thanks to our two-month circus ride, but judging from Senior's appearance and the small pieces of information I had heard, things weren't looking good.

We had to get back to work.

Instead of commenting, I merely nodded and inhaled another comforting whiff of the ocean before he walked away. Next to me, Amerie fidgeted in her chair.

"Have you heard anything from your brothers?" I asked.

She frowned. "Nothing good. Damascus fell to ISIS shortly after we left. They now control all of Syria." Her lips formed a thin line as she met my gaze. "Last I heard, Africa was their next target."

Emersyn shook her head and sighed. "People are going to have to start volunteering."

I almost snorted. "I'm not sure how much help a bunch of sniveling cowards who avoided the draft are going to be." I thought back to the protestors. "If anything, people are even more against the war than ever."

"If we want to win this, we need more people," Emersyn insisted.

Scowling, I crossed my arms.

Amerie leaned back in her seat. "America's military has proven time and time again we can hold our own against a larger force." Her gaze drifted over the three of us. "We're proof of that."

Emersyn frowned. "It doesn't matter how well the military holds its own; it can't be everywhere."

My scowl deepened.

I hated it, but she was right—we needed more people to enlist. "Yeah, well, in a few hours, we'll be back at work and able to help."

We had to be.

The soft murmurs in the room began to slowly trickle out. I watched as an elderly man in a dark suit entered the room. He took a seat at the head of the table and waited until only the sound of breathing filled the room.

My heartbeat began to pick up its pace, but I refused to acknowledge it as I sat taller in my chair. Breathing through my nose, I watched as Attorney General Franklin's dark eyes scanned the room of top government officials.

"Welcome, ladies and gentlemen. Thank you for meeting here today." He gave a small nod. "Before we begin today's proceedings, I would like us all to take a moment of silence for our troops deployed overseas."

I bowed my head and sent up a quick prayer. From the corner of my eye, I saw Emersyn grab her Star of David necklace while Dee finished making the sign of the cross.

Amerie tilted her head toward me and winked. "You got this," she mouthed.

I smiled as Attorney General Franklin began talking again.

"We will start today's hearing of the Damascus attack with the last testimony from SEAL Team One." He met my gaze as one of the committee members walked over with a Bible.

Placing my hand on the cover, I never broke eye contact with Attorney General Franklin as I was sworn in.

My neck and back burned from the gazes locked on me. The black sweater and slacks I wore suddenly felt too light, too exposing. I wished I could have worn my combat gear.

Surrounded by cream walls, government officials, and security guards, I should have felt safe, but my body knew better. Adrenaline pumped within me as if it sensed a fight was coming.

And a fight *was* coming…I knew a battlefield when I saw one.

Attorney General Franklin motioned for me to sit down. "If you would, please explain the events that happened the night of the Damascus attack."

Nodding, I leaned toward the small microphone. "Myself and two of my teammates were tasked with gathering intel from the Russian compound in Damascus. For a month we had successfully infiltrated the compound."

My mind flashed back to that last morning when Chief approached us for the move. I could still feel the nagging suspicion warning me not to go.

If only Chief had listened.

"We had also been providing security for the CIA case officers stationed in Damascus. The morning of the attack, we were asked to cover one of the case officers who was meeting a contact in the market." I frowned as the image of Will surrounded by a growing puddle of blood filled my mind.

Taking a short breath, I forced the memories away and continued. "Nothing about the meet felt right. We were just about to pull our case officer from the field when a suicide bomber detonated near him. The case officer was in critical condition and required extensive medical treatment."

I felt the urge to turn toward Chief and glare at him, but I resisted. "There were some…" I frowned as I struggled to find a politically correct term, "…differences of opinions on how to handle the situation, but it was decided to call in a Quick Reaction Force to extract the case officer. It was also decided that myself and the British soldier directly tailing the case officer would not participate in infiltrating the Russian compound that night."

Trying to contain my rage, I took a small breath before continuing. "Since we were not allowed to participate in the operation, the British soldier and I sat in the command center and watched from a live feed."

Hussein's hate-filled eyes clouded my vision. Even now, I could still feel his hostile aversion to women.

"We noticed one of the Syrian assets sneaking around the center. When we confronted him, we discovered he was trying to steal classified documentation."

Next to me, Amerie stiffened.

"At the same time, all contact with SEAL Team One was lost. I had a feeling the lost connection wasn't a coincidence, and I began questioning the Syrian. He informed us the Russians were offering money for any proof of Americans working in Damascus. He also admitted the Russians had learned of the American's involvement due to the hacking of an unsecure email server."

Soft murmurs and people shifting in their seats sounded behind me.

"When it became clear the mission was compromised, I immediately requested permission to assist SEAL Team One but was told to stand down."

Attorney General Franklin glanced down at some papers in front of him. "Chief Lynch states he never gave the order to stand down."

My lips pinched together. Narrowing my eyes, I shook my head. "We were told multiple times to stand down."

A loud huff came from across the room. I tilted my head just enough to glimpse Chief's red face glaring at me.

"We were never given the go-ahead to leave."

"Are you admitting you and those involved went against a direct order?" Attorney General Franklin asked.

"Yes, sir." I kept my head held high as I locked on to his gaze. "The mission was compromised. We had two SEALs, a CIA case officer, and a Syrian asset being tortured for information. We were the closest task force in the area. It was our job to get them out."

Out of the corner of my eye, I saw three heads nodding along with my statement. I felt strength from my sister's support.

"After we secured the Russian compound and retrieved all prisoners, we began sensitive site exploitation. This is when we confirmed that an unsecure email server had been hacked. I recognized Chief's email address from the reports I had sent him." I glanced at Emersyn for a second, before returning my gaze to Attorney General Franklin. "One of my teammates discovered the other address belonged to Madam President Carlisle." My hands clenched as I stared directly into Attorney General Franklin's dark eyes. "She used her maiden and middle name as an alias."

Feet shuffled and papers rustled behind me, but I ignored the noise. "When we returned to the base, we discovered the Syrian asset who had attempted to steal classified information had been released. We—"

"Who authorized the release?" Attorney General Franklin asked, cutting me off.

"Chief Lynch."

When Attorney General Franklin made no comment, I continued. "We knew the base was compromised and began an immediate evacuation for the case officers. An overhead ISR confirmed they would have safe travels until they met up with the QRF team that was en route for the injured case officer."

Emotion clogged my throat as I pictured Angelette and Nolan stepping forward to stay behind. I swallowed thickly.

"There was not enough room for everyone to leave in the van, so two case officers volunteered to stay behind."

Warm air from the vent drifted over my skin, sending me

back to Damascus. Back on the roof, bullets whizzed past my head as smoke and dust filled my lungs. Sweat ran down my back as the sound of an empty chamber filled my ears.

Amerie nudged my chair, snapping me from my nightmare.

I sat up straighter and cleared my throat. "We fought off the Syrian radicals for the next several hours. I had just fired my last round when air support from the British arrived."

Angelette's face flashed in my mind as numbness crept over my body. "We were loading onto the helo when one of the case officers was hit by enemy fire."

I glanced down at my microphone, refusing to let anyone in the room see my pain.

"Did you receive any American support?" Attorney General Franklin asked.

Meeting his gaze, I couldn't mask my anger as I spit out, "We didn't see an American plane until a few days later when we were leaving the Haifa base."

Attorney General Franklin regarded me for several pounding heartbeats before giving me a slight nod. "Thank you for your testimony." He glanced over the room. "This concludes all testimonies from the parties involved in the Damascus attack." He shuffled some papers on his desk before gazing at the crowd again. "Due to the recent allegations of possible Russian collusion in regard to the uranium deal made by the Carlisle administration…"

My muscles tensed.

No, no, no…

"…we cannot at this time form any decision regarding the actions and decisions of those involved in the Damascus attack. We will be conducting an extensive investigation to discover if these collusion allegations are linked to the events in Damascus."

I sucked in a breath. We couldn't sit on the sidelines that long.

Amerie met my gaze out of the corner of her eye. "We may not even still be the United States of America by the time they dig up all that information," she mumbled so low, I barely heard her.

My lips formed a thin line as I gave a curt nod. Across the room, I felt President Carlisle's heated glare. Ignoring the urge to face her, I kept my attention on Attorney General Franklin.

"As we have all seen and heard, we are not doing well in the war…" His gaze stopped on our table. "Since SEAL Team One has provided their testimonies, I am lifting their suspension."

A swell of relief rushed through me and I fought the urge to smile.

"Your country needs you four ladies to get back to work."

Attorney General Franklin spared the occupants in the room one last glance before he stood to leave. I waited until he exited the room before I let out the breath I had unconsciously held.

It was finally over.

The muscles in my mouth twitched. Sitting back in the plush leather, I let my smile escape its constraints.

"Damn fools."

And there goes my good mood…

Swiveling around in my chair, I met Chief's hostile glare. For a second, I watched the vein in his temple throb.

Resisting the urge to punch his cowardly, lying face, I plastered on a fake smile. "Always a pleasure to see you, Chief."

His face turned a shade darker as he took a step toward

me. I almost rolled my eyes at his pathetic attempt to intimidate me.

Was he serious?

"You're not fooling anyone," Chief spat. "When they discover that crap you spewed back there was nothing but lies, you four will spend the rest of your lives behind bars."

My face hardened.

"The truth always has a way of coming out," I growled as I stood up. Chief took a shaky step back, causing the edge of my lips to curve up. "My mama raised me right..." I glared into his beady eyes, "...*I* don't lie under oath."

The vein in Chief's temple continued to throb as he clenched his fists. "Damn fools," he muttered again. He turned his back on me and headed toward the door.

"Enjoy retirement!" Amerie called out in an overly bubbly voice.

Chief's footsteps faltered, but he didn't turn around.

I couldn't help but snicker as he tensely sulked from the room. Next to me, Dee folded her arms and glowered. "Anyone else would already be in jail for the things he did, but no, he gets a medal and is then politely asked to retire." She shook her head. "Some justice system."

Amerie nudged my shoulder. "Guess someone needs to tell the DOJ to man up and grow a pair, huh?"

The smirk appeared on my face before I could stop it. "I'm never going to live that down, am I?"

Emersyn and Dee laughed. "Never."

Chuckling, we walked toward the back of the room. Senior stood close to the door, wearing an expression similar to the one my mom wore when Charles and I misbehaved. His eyes remained on Amerie, who walked slowly behind me.

My lips struggled to keep from tipping up as I met his stern gaze. "She stayed on her best behavior..."

Senior shook his head like he would at a wayward daughter, which, in a way, that's what we were. Poor Pops. He had his hands full with the four of us.

Instead of commenting, he escorted us out into the main hallway, leading us away from the other officials. He stopped at the end of the hall and turned toward us.

"Congratulations."

He patted Emersyn on the shoulder while smiling at the rest of us. "I'll give you tonight to call your families to tell them the good news, and then in the morning, you'll be deploying."

He doesn't waste any time.

The thought made me want to smile.

Heck, I couldn't help myself…I smiled.

After two months of recovery, sitting on my butt, and playing the Washington two-step, I was *finally* getting to go back to work. Excited couldn't even begin to describe the feelings swirling within me.

Senior's warm eyes twinkled. "It's good to have you all back." The words had barely left his lips when his phone began buzzing. Frowning, he glanced at the screen. "We've needed you," he stated grimly before walking off to answer the call.

His tone caused some of my elation to wan, but my smile still remained. We were back!

Cinnamon filled my nose again as we walked down the Christmas tree hallway. The red and green lights continued their dance on the marble floors.

"I need to book a tour."

Emersyn was ogling the timeless paintings on the walls. Her round eyes left no doubt she had died and gone to history heaven.

Dee smirked. "Something tells me a tour wouldn't have had access to this part of the building."

Amerie snorted. "Yeah, we have an all-access backstage pass."

I bumped Emersyn's shoulder. "Perks of a secret hearing."

My gaze traveled over the paintings and architectural designs. I may not have been as enthused as Emersyn, but even I couldn't help but admire the heritage and prestige oozing from the walls.

Emersyn frowned. "I just wish we had a little more time."

"Don't worry, Bookie." I smirked at her. "I'm sure we'll get another chance to visit the White House."

Her lips tipped up. "You plan on taking an actual tour or having another backstage pass?"

I laughed. "With the four of us, I have no doubt it'll be backstage."

Chapter 4

OUTSIDE, THE WINTER AIR NIPPED AT MY CHEEKS CAUSING MY face to redden. My mind drifted back to Hell Week and the countless hours we spent in the freezing Pacific. A small smile flitted onto my lips. I could almost hear the incoming crash of the assaulting waves.

"Should we take a selfie?"

Amerie's taunting tone snapped me from my memories. I followed her line of vision to three young women with different sized baby bumps. They stood with their backs to the South Lawn, taking turns striking different poses with their war protest signs.

Dee snorted. "What would our caption be?"

Amerie glanced back at us with a wicked glint in her eyes. "Second Amendment-loving Deplorables." She smirked. "Hashtag 'Murica."

Laughing, I could only shake my head.

Snow began to trickle down and stick to the ground. Indulging my inner child, I stuck out my tongue and caught a few snowflakes while we walked down the sidewalk.

The sharp ring of a notification filled my ears as I watched the falling snow. I started to reach into my pocket when I caught a glimpse of Emersyn pulling her phone out.

Dodging an ice patch on the sidewalk, I walked with my head down as the harsh winter wind pushed against my face.

Even with my bundle of layers, my body still shivered against the assault.

Need. Hot. Chocolate.

"Kid…"

My eyes snapped toward Emersyn. Her furrowed brow and pursed lips had me scanning the area around us. Seeing nothing, I turned back toward her.

She wore a frown as she held her phone out to me.

I hesitated a heartbeat before I grabbed it and glanced over the breaking news alert. The muscles in my abdomen tightened as I read three cops in California had been shot and killed.

"Is your brother still stationed there?" Emersyn asked softly.

I closed my eyes and took a deep breath. "No. He went back to Texas two days ago."

Thank God.

I didn't even want to think about what would have happened had he not finished his training. Anger erupted inside me and I had to take a breath to fight it.

Amerie took the phone from me and scowled as she read the article. Pushing the phone back to Emersyn, she shoved her hands into her pockets and sighed. "The whole world is going crazy."

Frowning, I could only nod. An arctic breeze brought the scent of fried food. I looked toward the line of food trucks behind the protestors.

"Aw man." Amerie kicked a pile of snow as her lips puckered in a pout. "The one I wanted is leaving."

Trying hard not to laugh, I watched as the white truck pulled away from the line of vehicles. It headed toward the crowded street, accelerating at an alarming rate.

An uneasy feeling tingled down my spine. Something wasn't right.

Stopping, I stared at the truck.

From the corner of my eye, I could see my sisters' tense postures and narrowed gazes. The vehicle's rumbling grew as it picked up speed. It swerved to the left, jumping the curve.

Before I could shout out a warning, terrorized screams filled the air.

Running toward the speeding truck, I reached for my concealed gun, but my fingers brushed against skin.

"Damn it," Amerie cursed.

I didn't have to look to know she just came to the same realization as me; all of our guns were at the hotel.

We were weaponless.

Across from me, the food truck barreled through the crowd of protestors, sending bodies flying. Blood tainted its white hood as it veered toward the sidewalk.

Screams filled my ears as the truck raced toward us. Diving to the side of the walkway, a flash of red and white zoomed past. I felt a body land next to mine in the frozen snow. I rolled back onto my feet and met a pair of green eyes.

"You good?"

Amerie nodded.

Shots suddenly mixed in with the screaming. Security guards were firing at the truck that was speeding toward the back fence of the White House. The van slammed into the wrought iron and came to violent stop.

A sick feeling crawled down my spine as I watched a group of men slowly approach the van with their weapons drawn. Taking a few steps to the side, I craned my neck as far as I could and glimpsed movement through the passenger window. Tingles pricked along the base of my scalp as I took another step forward.

"Kid?"

Ignoring Amerie, I kept my gaze on the window. Through the broken glass, I could just make out the driver's bloody hand clutching something.

The air in my lungs squeezed out as I scrambled backwards.

"Get down!" I screamed, pulling Amerie down behind a bench with me.

The words had barely left my mouth when a loud blast erupted around us. A wall of heat rushed forward as snow and debris shot out. For a heartbeat, a piercing silence settled over the area, and then muffled screams filled my ringing ears.

People desperately ran from the scene, crying and shouting. A line of bloody, broken bodies created a path that led toward the growing flames of the blazing vehicle. A new set of officers began to surround the burning truck with their weapons drawn.

Across from me, Dee and Emersyn brushed off the snow covering their bodies.

Dee looked up and met my gaze. "Y'all okay?"

I nodded and waved a hand toward the blood dripping down the side of her arm. "Yeah, y'all?"

Dee gave a curt nod as she took in the area. Her eyes narrowed at the angry red flames. "I knew there was something shady about that truck."

Amerie grunted but kept her comments to herself. Approaching sirens mixed in with the agonized wailing. I glanced over the blood-covered ground and felt bile fill my mouth.

Emersyn caught my eye. "We're going to need a lot of ambulances here."

Frowning, I headed toward the closest body. "Help as many as you can."

Stepping over a large pool of blood, I knelt beside one of the women we had watched taking a selfie. Tears ran down her pale face as she clutched her bleeding leg. Her left arm was bent at an unnatural angle and a deep gash went from her temple down to her cheek.

"I'm here to help you," I said gently as I assessed her leg. It looked as if someone had used a butcher knife to slice her leg open. The deep cut made it possible to see the woman's tibia.

Taking off my scarf, I quickly tied a makeshift tourniquet.

"My friends?" the woman whimpered through clenched teeth.

I met her wide eyes for a moment before glancing around. Several yards to the right, Amerie leaned over one of the woman's friends. Her lips moved as she ripped off her coat and placed it on the woman's arm.

My gaze followed the trail of blood and then stopped on a lifeless body.

I bit my lip to keep from gasping. Swallowing hard, I forced myself to put on an expressionless mask as I took in the third woman's mangled body.

The way her arms and legs twisted at the wrong angles reminded me of a broken doll. Scarlet blood ran down her chest and pooled around the wooden stake protruding from her stomach. Splattered blood stained the top part of her sign.

Keeping my mask in place, I glanced back down at the woman's waiting gaze. Tears continued to stream down her pale face.

"One of my friends is helping now." I smiled, hoping my vague comment would put her at ease. I didn't want to lie to the woman, but as I scanned over her pale skin and wide eyes, I knew she wouldn't be able to handle the whole truth right now.

The sound of crunching snow drifted to my ears. I looked up to see a team of EMTs approaching with a stretcher. Rising to get out of the way, the woman reached up with her blood-covered hand and grasped mine. "Please don't leave me." Her wide eyes met mine as her blue lips trembled. "Please stay with me."

"You're going to be just fine." I squeezed the woman's hand. "Help is here."

The woman's eyes closed as she let out a sigh of relief. The action caused her to whimper and grimace in pain.

The EMTs reached us with the stretcher, and I stepped out of their way. "Patient's critical. She has about a twelve-inch laceration to her left leg, a broken left radius, some possible broken ribs, and probably some internal bleeding."

One of the EMTs checked my tourniquet. "Are you a doctor?"

I shook my head. "I've had some medical training."

The man's gaze narrowed slightly as understanding seeped into his features. He broke eye contact with me as he helped lift the woman on the stretcher. The woman cried out and slammed her eyes shut.

Shifting to the side, I made sure my body blocked her line of vision just in case she reopened her eyes. I didn't want her to see her friend's mangled body. Nobody should have to see that.

I waited until the stretcher reached the group of ambulances gathered by the police barricade before I moved. From the corner of my eye, I saw Emersyn walking toward me. Her coat was missing, and blood stained the long sleeves of her silk blouse.

"If it wasn't for all the snow, I'd think we were back in Damascus." She glanced around and sighed. "And all of the cell phones."

I turned my head to where she was looking and scowled. A group of people mingled around the injured, snapping pictures and crying as they recorded the brutal scene.

"You've got to be kidding me," I mumbled under my breath.

A young man without even a scratch walked past me, crying and blubbering in front of his phone. Clenching my teeth, I reached out and snagged the phone out of his hands.

"Hey!" he sputtered, his tears instantly vanishing.

"Get off your phone." I looked him up and down and shook my head in disgust. "You're not even hurt. You should be helping these people, not exploiting their suffering for your fifteen minutes of fame for likes and comments."

His wide eyes took in the blood covering my hands and torso, and his Adam's apple bobbed. The blood drained from his face as he clutched his stomach.

Rolling my eyes, I shoved the phone into his clammy hands. "You've got to be kidding me," I said as I stormed off toward the injured.

Emersyn jogged to catch up to me. Turning my head, I met her scowl. "Can you believe that snowflake pansy?" I shook my head and sighed. "What has our society become?"

We reached a woman curled in the fetal position beside a pile of snow. Emersyn knelt beside her, taking her pulse. After a few seconds, she met my gaze and shook her head.

Rubbing the back of my neck, I sighed. "This isn't supposed to happen in America."

Emersyn stood up and folded her arms. "Do you think this was ISIS or white supremacists or Antifa?"

For a second, I couldn't respond. Numbness swept over my body. What was happening to our country?

I never thought I'd live to see the day where we had to

ask if this act of terrorism came from a radical Jihadist or a radical American.

Clenching my fists, I glared at the burning food truck.

A cold breeze pushed my hair away from my face. Next to me, Emersyn shivered. Shrugging out of my coat, I handed it to her.

She shook her head. "I'm fine."

Ignoring her protest, I shoved my coat into her blood-covered hands. "I at least have a sweater on, you've got that silk crap."

"Thanks," she mumbled as she pushed her arms through the sleeves.

I chewed on my bottom lip and gazed at the red and white ground. "I honestly don't know who's behind this." A sick feeling swelled inside of me. "It could have been any of them."

Emersyn frowned. "If this was radical Americans, this could be the start of a civil war."

I met her worried gaze briefly before glancing back at the carnage. "We'd better start praying that doesn't happen." I turned back toward Emersyn and muttered, "There's no way America can survive a civil war *and* a world war."

Chapter 5

ENDING MY PHONE CALL WITH MY PARENTS, I LOOKED AT Amerie and quirked an eyebrow at the grin she was fighting off.

"How is it that we're always in the middle of trouble?"

I smiled humorlessly. "Must be a talent." Plopping down in the chair next to her, I ran a hand through the rat's nest on my head.

"Call home that bad?" Amerie asked.

Sighing, I shook my head. "They're just worried about me." I pulled a hair tie off of my wrist and tried to tame my wild locks. "I think my parents thought I'd be coming home for a little bit. Especially after this little ordeal."

I released another sigh and glanced out the dirty window. "I just hate making them worry." I could handle anything, but hearing my parents get choked up…nothing cut deeper.

Amerie nodded. "Yeah, that's the hardest part." She shifted in her chair and started tapping her fingers against her thigh.

"You hear anything about your brothers?"

Amerie turned her head toward the window. "They told Mom they're fine…"

My gaze drifted down to her fingers as they picked up their tempo.

"But that's a lie." Her drumming abruptly stopped. She let

out a long sigh and then slowly turned to face me. "We were in Syria. We know the truth."

Her green eyes lacked their usual spark as I held her gaze. I tried to think of something to say to ease her worries, but I knew no words would bring her peace of mind.

Like she said, we knew the truth.

Amerie leaned her head back into the chair's headrest. "I just wish it was me there and not them."

"Don't worry," I assured her as Emersyn and Dee entered the small office room, "pretty sure we'll be there soon."

Dee sat down next to me and winced when her arm brushed against mine. An angry red gash marred her caramel skin.

"Never thought I'd be dodging car bombs in Washington," she mumbled.

I shook my head. The whole world had gone crazy.

The door creaked open and a pair of heavy footsteps stomped in. Senior strode past us and took his seat at the head of the table. His warm eyes traveled over each of our faces.

A scowl flashed on his face when he noticed Dee's injured arm. "Every time there is trouble, the four of you always seem to be in the middle of it." He cocked an eyebrow. "Why is that?"

The muscles in my mouth strained, but I resisted the urge to smirk.

Senior's gaze landed on me. "And don't say it's a talent, Connally."

Shaking my head, I let my smirk make its appearance. Senior's talents never ceased to amaze me. The man had superpowers.

A hint of amusement sparked in Senior's eyes, but the humor didn't last long. He sat up straighter in his chair and clicked a remote. Images from the truck assault popped onto the projector screen.

"Today's incident has been confirmed as an ISIS attack." The screen switched to a blurry video of a group of masked radicals waving a flag, cheering and praising the driver's success. "ISIS claimed responsibility shortly after the driver killed himself."

I clenched my fists. Those assholes were going to pay.

Keeping my face an expressionless mask, I continued listening to Senior. "President Macleod wants to send Syria a message."

Out of the corner of my eye, I saw Amerie's lips twitch up.

"An airstrike is in route to the radicals' two strongholds: Aleppo and Damascus." Senior scowled. "The British have been performing their own air raids over the past few weeks, trying to flush out those cockroaches, but somehow they keep finding ways to burrow deeper in their infested holes."

My stomach tightened, and I found myself leaning forward in my seat.

"Several teams have already been deployed to assist the Marines cleaning out in Aleppo." Senior met my gaze. "We need another team in Damascus."

The need for retribution hummed within me. Somewhere in that hellhole lived Angelette's murderer.

"With your history, several officials did not believe it was appropriate for you four to return..."

"We can do it," I blurted before I could stop myself.

Other than a stern look, Senior ignored my outburst. "You all know the city better than anyone." He took the time to look each of us in the eye. "You have a job, and you will get it done."

A shot of adrenaline surged through my bloodstream. Senior gave the best pep talks.

I was beyond ready to kick some ISIS ass.

Trying to control the energy coursing through me, I leaned back in my chair and watched as Senior walked to the back of the room. He opened a filing cabinet and pulled out four small boxes. My eyebrows pulled together as he placed a box in front of each of us.

"We never had time for a proper graduation, but you have all earned the right to be called a SEAL."

My lips parted as my gaze moved from Senior to the small box. Slowly, I lifted the lid and revealed a golden eagle holding a trident.

Emotions swelled inside of me.

I ran a finger over the trident's prongs and smiled. My gaze traveled from my trident back to Senior's brown eyes.

"Time to get to work."

Chapter 6

A RELIEVED BREATH OOZED FROM MY MOUTH AS THE HELO touched down. A snicker drifted over me.

"Still scared of flying?"

I glared at Amerie. "Still claustrophobic?" I shot back.

The smirk vanished from her cheerful face as she narrowed her eyes at me. I grabbed my bag and smirked at her pursed lips.

Chuckling, Dee's shoulder brushed against mine as she hopped out. "You two…" Her laughter abruptly broke off as she covered her nose and grimaced. "Man, I forgot how bad it smelled here."

My own nose wrinkled. "Beats the snow."

"I don't know about that," Emersyn mumbled as she jogged past.

The wind from the chopper whipped our hair around as the blades began to slowly wind down. Through the wall of dust, I could just make out the edges of a tall man.

Squinting, I peered through the haze and met a pair of dark chocolate eyes. "T.R.?"

His white teeth flashed at me. "About time you four got back to work."

I beamed as he gave my shoulder a pat. "Good to be back."

T.R. led us through a set of doors and down a plywood hallway. "This is one of our new bases in Syria. We're about fifteen minutes outside of Damascus." He waved a hand at a few wooden doors. "This is your barracks, two to a room. You can toss your things and then follow me."

I opened the door closest to me and found two small cots with grey blankets filling the space. I eyed the bare walls and then side-stepped into the glorified closet.

"Looks like we got the Ritz again," Dee mumbled.

I dropped my gear onto a bed and shrugged. Tilting my head, I met Dee's gaze. "Good to be back."

A small smile tugged at the corners of her mouth. "Yeah, it really is."

I tied my hair back into a better ponytail and joined the others waiting in the hallway. Dee's feet had barely crossed the threshold when T.R. started ushering us down the hall again.

Amerie hummed *Bad Company* as her gaze drifted over the closed doors. T.R. made it past the chorus before he glanced back with an arched eyebrow. "I wasn't aware I bought a ticket to the Legacy concert."

She gave him a small smile. "Sorry, it's stuck in my head."

T.R.'s mouth twitched but he didn't say anything. Our boots echoed down the empty hallway. The smell of dust and plywood filled my nose as a small line of sweat trickled down my back.

My lips tugged up.

It's good to be back.

I had missed the heat.

I didn't care what Emersyn said, you could get used to the smell here, but dealing with all that freezing snow and ice in Washington…way worse.

T.R. led us past the chow hall and turned down another hallway before walking into a small meeting room. Several rows of folding metal chairs stood in front of a white projector screen. A table with small buildings on top of it stood next to the screen. My gaze darted to the nicest building on the table. Compared to the others, it resembled the Taj Mahal.

I sucked in a breath.

Amerie bumped my shoulder. "Can't believe that thing is still standing," she whispered.

I couldn't either.

I looked up at the screen T.R. had turned on. A man with beady eyes and a dark, grizzly beard glared back at me. Chill bumps formed across my skin as another pair of similar eyes flashed in my mind.

"Abdul al Jurrah." T.R. clicked a remote and several different frames of Abdul popped up. "He is the older brother of Khalid al Jurrah."

My fingers fisted as I stared into Abdul's dark eyes. Next to me, Amerie stiffened. Her fingers began to tap against her leg in a slow, deadly rhythm.

Dee glared at the images as Emersyn walked over and pulled out a chair. Folding her arms, she leaned back and stared thoughtfully at the screen. "He's why we're here."

Although she hadn't voiced her statement as a question, T.R. answered anyway. "Yes."

The screen changed again to a group of rundown buildings riddled with battle scars. Off in the distance, I noticed several demolished vendor stands.

"Our intel has tracked him to what I believe you all called the Bermuda Triangle." T.R. changed the screen again to Abdul with five other bearded men surrounding a young British soldier.

Bile filled my throat.

"This squirrelly son of a bitch has killed twenty British

soldiers in the past month alone. He never stays in one place for long."

"So we need to move on him tonight," Dee stated in a cold tone.

T.R. nodded and moved toward the Damascus model. I glanced over his head at Emersyn's furrowed brow. She briefly met my gaze before walking to the table.

T.R. pointed to a small convoy west of what used to be our Bermuda. "A group of Marines will be doing house searches here." He pointed north of the Bermuda at a British flag. "And over here, a group of Brits will be taking care of the north end houses."

I looked to the east side where several buildings laid toppled over. Moving toward the south, a few buildings stood, but several were knocked over as well.

Emersyn flicked her wrist toward the end of the table. "You think he's on the south side?"

T.R. nodded. "We've had him cornered before, but the man is smart."

Frowning, I briefly made eye contact with Amerie before turning back to T.R. "So he's just like his brother."

Emersyn walked around the table and folded her arms. "He'll be expecting an attack. He'll have a way out." She pointed to the rubble. "If I were him, this is where I'd escape to. It's on the outskirts of the Bermuda and a direct shot out of town if he has a vehicle waiting."

Amerie leaned against the table and cocked an eyebrow. "Out in the open?"

Emersyn glanced at her. A wicked glint appeared in her eyes as she tried to fight a smirk.

My gaze shifted between the two as realization slowly dawned on me.

"That sneaky fox." I folded my arms and shook my head. "He's using underground tunnels to avoid us."

Emersyn nodded while Amerie groaned.

Fighting the urge to smirk at Amerie, I turned toward T.R. "Have the Marines run across any of these tunnels during their searches?"

He shook his head. "None so far, but this is the first wave actually in the city. We just broke through the outskirts last night."

I nodded but kept my gaze on the Damascus model. Emersyn had to be right.

Amerie pointed to a tall building across from the east lot. "I'd have a good vantage point here."

T.R. folded his arms across his thick chest. "That's a good spot." He grabbed a small figurine and placed it on the building. "Let's get to work."

For the next several hours, we constructed and tweaked a plan to flush out the conniving fox. By the time T.R. nodded his approval, I felt like I could perform the mission in my sleep.

His gaze met mine and then shifted over my sisters. "Get some rest and then be ready to head out."

Without another word, he left the room. The familiar tingle of adrenaline hummed within me, begging to be let loose. I couldn't wait for my hit. It had been too long.

Folding her arms, Emersyn peered down at the model.

"What do you think, Bookie? Will this work?"

Her lips pursed. "There are a lot of factors and moving parts…" The thoughtful glint in her eyes transformed into determination as she met my gaze. "We'll definitely be sending those ISIS a-holes a message."

A wicked grin pulled up the corners of my mouth. "Hooyah."

Chapter 7

Smoke and dust clogged my lungs, making it difficult to breathe. Dodging a pile of rubble, a click sounded in my ear.

"Secure on the east," Amerie announced.

My gaze swept over the deserted dusty street. "Two klicks from target," I whispered.

Behind me, the soft footsteps of Emersyn and Dee broke the night's silence. From the corner of my eye, I caught Dee shaking her head as she stepped over a slab of concrete.

"Can you believe this?" She sighed. "Those little kids used to play over here, and now…" She didn't finish her sentence, not that she needed to. The architectural graveyard said more than enough.

Frowning, I slinked past another pile of rubble. All around us, shattered walls and broken beams littered the ground. Lying trapped under a chipped cement block, a little girl's doll stared vacantly at the destruction.

Anger tightened my throat.

If I hadn't seen it with my own eyes, I wouldn't have believed buildings and homes stood here two months ago. Years' worth of memories and time…just gone, demolished into a pile of dust and rocks.

"Hopefully, they got out in time…" Emersyn gnawed on her lower lip as she stared at the doll.

I recalled all the times the locals had vanished just before trouble came, as if they possessed a sixth sense for impending danger.

"I'm sure they did, Bookie," I finally answered. "These people know the signs. They know when to get out of town." I kept my gaze forward as we continued making our way through the rubble. "This is their world."

Before she could reply, a cloud of dust picked up a few yards in front of us. Melting into the shadows of a half-standing wall, I lined my scope on the movement.

I eased my finger away from the trigger as a small, mangy dog limped across the street before disappearing into a broken home. Releasing a breath, I waited a few more heartbeats.

"Clear," Dee whispered.

I nodded. "Clear."

Our hushed breathing brought the only sign of life to the desolate street. Not even the stars or the ever-constant gunfire wanted to present itself to this part of town. It was as if the entire city of Damascus had forgotten this section still existed.

As the grey compound came into sight, I eased behind a broken half wall and scanned the area.

Most of the compound's wall lay scattered across the street and its dirt-covered yard. The majority of its buildings leaned dangerously close to the ground or displayed gaping craters for walls. Only one building near the back appeared strong enough to house people.

Emersyn inched next to me and bumped my shoulder. She tilted her head toward the least battle worn building.

I nodded. "Target in sight."

Off in the distance, I could finally hear the soft rumble of sporadic gunfire. I felt rather than saw Dee edge closer to my other side.

"Ready?" she asked.

I gave a curt nod. My muscles tensed as my finger hovered close to the trigger. I darted through the broken wall, and winced as concrete and glass crunched noisily underneath my boots. Reaching the building's door, I took point and scanned the windows for any threats.

"Clear," I whispered as Dee ran her hand over the doorframe.

"Clear," Emersyn answered further down from me.

"This thing's a piece of crap," Dee mumbled as she pulled out her Military Halligan Bar.

I eyed the metal door that looked like a strong wind could have knocked it off its hinges. "Good," I pulled out the small sledgehammer I'd brought for the mission, "makes our job a whole lot easier."

Sweat dotted Dee's forehead as her thin fingers quickly positioned the Halligan head just below the door's handle.

I felt Emersyn move closer behind me just before Dee's gaze met mine. Wordlessly, I slammed the top of my hammer against the flat striking face of the Halligan. It took two powerful hits before one of the hinges clattered to the ground, allowing Dee to wrench open the door.

Emersyn bounded past us, her muzzle ready to line up any possible threats. Strapping our tools back into place, Dee and I darted through the entryway a few steps behind her.

Silence and darkness greeted us.

My finger hovered over the trigger as I crept down the hall. Shattered glass and chunks of concrete covered the floor. Stepping lightly, I slinked into one of the front rooms.

"Clear," Dee and Emersyn whispered.

"Clear," I chimed in. Reaching the end of the hall, I rounded the corner.

A set of crumbling stairs loomed by the back wall. Broken

drywall and plaster littered the concrete floor. Toward the end of the hall, a dim light seeped out from under a closed door. Hushed male voices drifted down to where I stood.

A wicked grin popped onto my face.

My breathing slowed down as a calm determination ignited within me. My muscles coiled, ready to spring.

Still several strides away from the door, the light began to grow, filling the end of the hall with a golden glow.

A man stepped out into the hallway but kept his eyes on the other occupants in the room. Trying to blend into the remaining shadows, I lined my sights on the man but held my fire. I wanted him to shut the door before I took him out.

The last thing I wanted was to alert the others to our presence. We needed to take Abdul—dead or alive—not give him time to escape in his underground tunnel because this man blew our cover.

"Let's please do this the easy way," I mumbled.

The man continued to stand in the doorway, gazing into the room. He gave a small nod and then turned toward us with his hand wrapped around the doorknob.

He took a small step, pulling the door slowly with him. The shadows trickled back in, inching over the glow. The man's body became divided in half shadow, half golden light. He took another step and tensed.

I pressed into the wall and tried to become invisible.

Leaning forward, the man's eyes narrowed as he glared at my hiding spot.

I suppressed a sigh. *Always the hard way.*

He opened his mouth at the same time his hand twitched toward the rifle slung over his shoulder.

I squeezed my trigger, and he dropped before he could utter a sound. Shouts filled the small hallway, followed by pounding feet above our heads. I darted into an open room just as a spray of bullets descended upon us.

A group of four men raced down the set of stairs, yelling and firing a relentless storm of bullets.

"Sheba!" I shouted over the gunfire as I took aim at a large man lunging out of the doorway. "Take them out!" I squeezed my trigger and watched the large man crash to the ground.

"Got 'em," Dee stated calmly as she lined her grenade launcher on the insurgents.

A small pop sounded behind me and then a deafening roar stabbed my eardrums. The walls trembled as smoke and dust clogged my lungs. Squinting through the haze, four motion-less bodies lay broken in a pile of rubble. Above them, a large empty space occupied where the middle part of the stairs used to be.

A bullet skimmed the top of my helmet, and I lurched back further behind my doorframe. Rotating my sights over, I lined another man in my crosshairs, but before I could pull my trigger, he crumbled to the ground, falling beside the large man.

Out of the corner of my eye, I saw Emersyn glancing toward me.

"You good?"

I nodded. "Yeah."

Loud male voices and movement came from the room, but no one rushed out of the door with a gun. A heartbeat went by before I eased out of my room.

"Move forward."

With Emersyn and Dee shadowing my movements, I darted toward the doorway and used the frame as a partial shield. Standing beside me, Dee lobbed a grenade over my shoulder into the room.

Shouting briefly filled my ears before it being drowned out by a resounding boom. Smoke poured into my nose as I bounded into the room.

Three lifeless bodies lay strewn across the concrete floor. Through the haze, a flash of dark fabric caught my eye before it disappeared behind a corner.

"Target's on the move."

"Copy that," Emersyn and Dee answered.

Dee and I pressed forward while Emersyn secured the other section of the room. I rounded the corner and lunged back as bullets sprayed down on me.

Wall fragments dug into my exposed skin as the bullets shattered the feeble plaster. Dee crouched low next to me. She met my gaze briefly and gave a slight nod.

Gritting my teeth, I leaned my barrel around the corner and fired a few rounds at the man shielded behind an over-turned table. The spray of bullets returned, forcing me to take a step back. Below me, Dee inched forward. The torrent of bullets slowed, and I heard a few grunts mix in with the gunfire.

"Sheba, execute."

Still in a crouch, Dee pushed off the wall with me following right behind her. I had barely cleared the corner's shelter when a single shot rang out and the man slumped to the ground. Not slowing my stride, I moved past his body and glimpsed the top of Abdul's head as he descended down a set of hidden stairs to an underground tunnel. I moved my crosshairs toward Abdul just as two men pushed a large metal filing cabinet down on the trap door.

"Target's heading your way, Legacy." I hoped. "He's on the move in the tunnels."

Sweat dripped down my soot-covered face as I lined one

of the remaining men in my sights. He fell to the ground just before his companion.

"Clear," Emersyn called out.

"Clear," Dee stated a few feet away from me.

I was about to announce my side of the room was secure when one of the men started wriggling. I raised my barrel and lined the back of the man's head in my site as he tried to crawl away.

My stomach clenched.

Biting my cheek, I took a deep breath and jerked my muzzle down. The man may have been a savage scumbag, but I couldn't make myself shoot him in the back. Killing the wounded like that…just the thought of it made me feel just as vile and cruel as the sadistic radicals.

"I've got one prisoner to contain," I called out as I eased toward the wounded man.

From the corner of my eye, I saw Dee heading my way. She'd have my back if he tried anything stupid.

As soon as the thought popped into my mind, the man rolled over, clutching a grenade in his hands. His eyes narrowed to slits as he locked on to my gaze.

Dee's warning shout filled my ears just as the man pulled out the grenade's pin. My heart seemed to stop as I dove to the side toward the only shelter near me, an overturned stuffed chair.

Concrete and plaster rained down on my body as my ears rang with an annoying buzzing sound. I released a shaky breath before brushing off some of the debris covering my torso.

"Kid?" Dee yelled.

I leaned back against the floor and took a second breath to slow my heart rate. "I'm good," I answered slowly.

She rushed to my side and checked over my body. Other than a slight sting in my cheek, I felt fine.

"I can't believe you just have a little cut." Dee shook her head and quickly made the sign of the cross.

I let out a breathless laugh. "Yeah, me either." That had been way too close for comfort.

"Come on." She stuck out her hand and helped me to my feet.

I glanced at the filing cabinet covering the trap door and groaned. A large pile of rubble pinned it down.

"So much for chasing the fox," I grumbled.

I had no doubt Abdul had planned this. As much as I hated to admit it, the man was good.

As Emersyn radioed the news to T.R., Dee looked around the area and scowled. "I guess the rest is on Legacy and the others."

She tried to hide it, but I could hear the anger and reluctance in her voice. I felt the same way. I hated that Abdul was able to get past us. It ticked me off more than anything.

"Let's start sensitive site exploitation," I instructed.

Dee kicked a pile of concrete and mumbled something low under her breath.

Shouldering my M4, I walked toward the filing cabinet. "The quicker we get this done, the quicker we can head to the east side of town and help."

Dee gave a slight shake of her head, but other than a slight huff, she kept the rest of her thoughts to herself as she started moving pieces of rubble.

Sweat dripped down my face, creating dark spots on the cement. Huffing, I pushed a large chunk of concrete off the metal drawers and let out a relieved breath. I pulled on the drawer and flicked through some folders.

"Anything?" Dee asked.

I scanned through the blank pages and frowned. "Nope."

Emersyn walked through the door carrying a laptop. "Found something."

"Well, at least we didn't totally flop on the mission," Dee grumbled.

"Anything else?" I asked Emersyn.

"Nah, just a bunch of empty rooms."

Nodding, I sat down and leaned against what was left of the wall to gain some leverage as I tried to shove the filing cabinet with my legs. It barely moved an inch before my legs gave out.

Dee bent down and assessed the area before shaking her head. "Save your energy. The blast knocked out all of the support beams here. There's no way for us to follow Abdul through the tunnel."

Frowning, I wiped the sweat from my brow. "Alright, site's secure. Let's head out."

The ground under my feet crunched as we jogged down the street. The familiar burn in my legs greeted me as we made our way through the deserted area.

Sporadic gunfire filled the night air.

"Anything, Legacy?"

If Abdul took the tunnel somewhere else, the entire mission would be a bust. My stomach clenched at the thought.

"Not…" Amerie paused.

I glanced sideways at Emersyn and Dee, my fingers tightening around my M4.

"I've got movement," Amerie whispered.

Static filled my ear as sweat trickled down my face.

Muffled shouts drifted with the breeze, followed by a fired shot.

My stride slowed as I glanced around. Out of the corner of my eye, I noticed Emersyn and Dee doing the same.

"Target secure."

I breathed a sigh of relief. "Good work, Legacy."

Dee nodded as we returned to our faster pace. "I feel like I'm back in BUD/S," she huffed.

I snorted. "BUD/S was way worse."

Even in the dark, I couldn't miss Emersyn's smile. "You only say that 'cause you couldn't ever beat me on our runs."

I smirked. "You didn't beat me every time."

Emersyn pouted as she recalled the time I had finally tied with her. Before she could make a retort, we turned past a toppled building and met the rest of our group.

Hushed murmurs surrounded me as I eased behind the figures circling the fallen body. Someone laid out a body bag and then whisked Abdul away.

From the radio, a familiar voice pierced my ears. "Site is secure. Exfil."

I watched as T.R. strolled out of the small, dilapidated building with a sack I assumed was filled with intel. His chocolate eyes met mine, and he gave a curt nod.

"Good work."

I barley kept the grimace off of my face. Nothing hurt my pride more than knowing Abdul had outmaneuvered me.

Spurts of distant gunfire grabbed my attention. Tightening my hold on my weapon, I quickly made my way to the convoy waiting to haul us back to base.

Amerie jogged over and hopped onto the seat next to me. "It never stops," she mumbled.

I glanced around and shook my head. "Couldn't imagine."

She frowned. "Different world."

Gravel and sand flew out as the vehicle lurched forward.

Bracing my feet on the floorboard, I tightened my muscles and tried to keep from falling forward.

As my body adjusted to T.R.'s driving, I stared out the dusty window at the passing buildings. A faded, threadbare sheet flapped in the gentle wind, revealing a sleeping family huddled on top of thin blankets.

Sighing, I tore my gaze away from the family.

Two months. It had only been two months.

Emersyn shifted in her seat next to me. She clutched at the Star of David that hung around her neck. "People in America don't know how good they have it."

Frowning, I shook my head. "No, they don't."

We passed a small child huddled under a torn cloth, sound asleep on the broken sidewalk.

Having to grow up in something like this...I couldn't even imagine. Things in America weren't perfect, but compared to so many places, we definitely had it made.

The vehicle tilted to the side as T.R. attempted to drive like he was starring in *The Fast and The Furious*. I threw my hand out to keep from ramming the front seat. I glanced back out the window to see how much longer of a drive we had left with the Dominic Toretto wannabe.

A tall building loomed several yards from the street. The air from my lungs whooshed out as I recognized the structure.

"Oh my..." Emersyn leaned over and sucked in a breath.

"Wow, I can hardly recognize it," Dee mumbled.

The Russian's compound, or what used to be the compound, lay scattered in heaps. What had been the Taj Mahal of Damascus was now just another part of the rotting architectural cemetery.

The wall surrounding the house lay in crumbled blocks. Dirt patches and weeds surrounded the fallen flagpole and scattered pieces of marble. The whole front of the building looked as if someone had reached in and grabbed it. Even in the dark, I could see the broken chandelier lying in shattered ruins.

Amerie let out a low whistle. "No one's safe in Damascus."

Chapter 8

I PUSHED MY LEGS HARDER, FASTER.

Come on, Greer…run

Pumping my arms, I forced my weary muscles to accelerate. Behind me, heavy breathing filled my ears. Dust kicked up around me as I rounded the building and raced past a parked Humvee.

I glanced down at my watch and smiled. "Not too shabby."

Glancing back, I waited for Amerie to catch up. Breathing hard and red-faced, she rushed past me and skidded to a halt. She raised her hands over her head and walked toward me.

"Just wait till we get back to the water. I'll swim circles around you," she said, panting.

Smirking, I did a dramatic look around the sand. "I don't see any water around here."

Amerie rolled her eyes but didn't say anything as she tried to slow her breathing down. I glanced at the Punisher symbol spray painted on her cut-off tee. A crooked crown sat at an angle on top of the skull.

Amerie noticed my gaze and gave me a pointed look. "I still say our nickname should be the Bad Bitches," she said as she walked toward the gym area. "I mean, how badass would that be?"

The symbol she had made for us honoring her uncle was

badass, and I agreed with her. But then my thoughts traveled to Emersyn.

"It'd be badass until Bookie called us the Bad Bs or BBs. Do you really want to be called the BBs?" I asked with an arched eyebrow.

Her mouth pinched together, and she grunted something low under her breath. Chuckling, I walked into the makeshift gym and found Dee and Emersyn lifting weights. My gaze traveled back to the tilted crown.

"What about the Queen Bs?" I asked as I stretched my arms.

Amerie rocked her head back and forth as if she was testing out the name in her head. After a few seconds, she gave a nod as her lips slowly curved up in a wicked smile. "I like it."

"Like what?" Emersyn asked as she racked her weights.

"Our nickname." She held out her shirt, proudly showing off the crowned Punisher. "Queen Bs."

Dee beamed. "I love it."

Emersyn nodded. "Me too."

"You think Santa can bring us some shirts like that for Christmas?" I asked as Amerie walked to the bench press.

Amerie grunted as she started her reps. "Hell no. You three are getting a bunch of coal this year."

Laughing, I finished stretching and breathed deeply. Sweat dotted my forehead as I switched places with Amerie and started lifting the weighted bar.

My shoulder ached a little from the exertion but otherwise performed admirably.

I smiled.

No bullet wound was going to keep me from my sisters and work.

Footsteps drifted into the workout area, and I lifted my

head to see flaming red hair walking toward us. A wide smile immediately popped onto my face when I recognized the splattered mess of freckles.

"Damn. Two months off and you start sweating from a little ol' workout?"

Bounding to my feet, I walked into Rilynn's outstretched arms.

"Good to see you too, Red."

Behind her, Valerie and Ziana walked in with wide grins. After everyone received their welcome back hugs, Rilynn smirked. "Heard you guys were going to be around, should have known it was y'all taking out that asshole."

Amerie grinned. "Who else would it have been?"

Valerie and Ziana rolled their eyes.

"Same ol' Legacy." Rilynn snorted. She met my gaze, and her smile slowly turned down as she became serious. "Heard about what happened with you all, glad you four are finally back at work." She strolled over to a chair and plopped down. "We could really use all the help we can get."

Valerie folded her arms and nodded. "Yeah, especially since we'll be heading out tonight."

Dee and I exchanged looks. Something in Valerie's tone had my stomach twisting into knots.

"Where are you guys heading?" Emersyn asked.

"Russia." Rilynn leaned forward, placing her elbows on her knees. "Things are getting bad there too."

Ziana walked over and sat down next to Rilynn. "Yeah, apparently, our French allies need some backup." She scowled. "So, we get to freeze our assess off while you lucky ladies get to enjoy the warm weather."

I laughed. "Sucks for y'all."

Ziana's eyes narrowed at me. "Senior knew your Texas

butt wouldn't be tough enough to handle it. That's why he's sending us."

Shrugging, I laughed again. The thought of having to spend any time in Russia during the winter made me want to cringe. I couldn't find it in myself to deny her statement. Damascus may have been hell, but I'd rather be stuck in a fiery hell than a frozen one.

"So, Russia, Africa, Syria…" Emersyn arched an eyebrow. "Any other strongholds?"

I could hear the wheels in Emersyn's brain starting to turn with the new information. The past two months, we'd been left in the dark regarding intel. Other than what the public was privy to on the news, we didn't have any idea what was going on behind the scenes.

"Not that I know of. All of the Middle East is basically jihadist central. It's the worst in Syria. Africa is starting to gain some movement," Valeri said.

Rilynn nodded. "Last I heard, Niger, Mali, and Libya have fallen and their surrounding countries are close."

I met Rilynn's gaze. "Russians?"

"They are providing a lot of support."

"And our support?"

Rilynn shook her head and sighed. "Most of Europe has joined, but their numbers are low like ours. China is still on the fence about joining."

I sighed. We needed more numbers. A lot more.

"The Irish have been kicking ass though," Ziana chimed in.

I smirked. "My people know how to fight."

Soft chuckles disturbed the heavy solemnness hanging in the air. I soaked in the brief laughter before the weighted seriousness settled back.

"What about the whispers of North Korea?" Emersyn asked.

Rilynn shook her head. "Nothing has been reported. If they are helping, they are being very careful about staying in the dark."

Ziana moved a rock with the toe of her boot. "I say they're helping."

I turned toward her and arched an eyebrow.

"Help is coming from somewhere. Every stronghold has an unlimited amount of ammunition and weapons. We've lost ground a few times just because we can't stay stocked as long as they can." She glowered. "The only other place that makes sense to have the time and manpower to be doing something like that is North Korea."

Out of the corner of my eye, I saw Emersyn's lips pinch together. She crossed her arms and went into her thinking mode.

Dee glanced at Emersyn for a second before meeting Rilynn's gaze. "How have things been here?" she asked.

Rilynn sighed. "It's…Damascus," she finally answered.

I nodded in complete understanding.

Rilynn scratched at the crook of her elbow, where a long, jagged cut wrapped around her arm. She caught my stare and placed her hands back in front of her. "We've been working with the Marines, cleaning houses out. The goal is to wash out the radicals."

She took a deep breath and glanced at Valerie and Ziana, both of whom had their eyes on the ground, chewing on their lower lips.

Amerie narrowed her eyes at the two of them. "What?"

Rilynn looked at Amerie and sighed. "It's just a different world here."

None of us said anything.

I kept my face expressionless and waited for Rilynn to voice the images that haunted her. But I knew they were the same images that haunted me.

"You're preaching to the choir," Amerie stated with her usual charm.

Valerie licked her lips and shook her head. "We heard about some of the things you've all seen." Her eyes darted down as she took a deep breath. "Things have changed…"

"They're a lot worse," Ziana finished in a cold tone.

Uneasiness fell over the room. Dee pushed herself off the wall and walked toward Rilynn. "How different?" she asked.

Rilynn's lips turned down as her eyes adopted a haunted look. "Kids."

I felt my forehead scrunch up.

Wearing the same expression as me, Amerie crossed her arms. "What do you mean, kids?"

Rilynn sighed. "That's the new tactic of these assholes." She shook her head and leaned back in her chair. "Kids as young as five and seven are in the streets taking out soldiers, teenagers are blowing themselves up trying to take out one of our units."

"I didn't sign up to kill children…" Ziana ran her hand across the back of her neck. "But if we don't, a lot of Americans and Brits die."

"This is just a shitty place," Valerie mumbled as she kicked a small rock.

My mouth parted and then closed. I had seen some horrible things during my time in Damascus, but at least I hadn't had to kill any kids. I couldn't imagine having to make that decision.

Looking over at Dee, Emersyn, and Amerie, I knew it was a feeling none of us wanted to experience.

Please, Lord, don't put me in that position.

Amerie's gaze met mine as she walked over to my side. "Some pretty messed up shit," she said.

I nodded. "This whole place is."

When Amerie didn't say anything, I gave her a side glance. She stared intensely into my eyes.

"What?" I asked.

She arched an eyebrow. "You ready for this?"

My face hardened. Straitening up, I squared my shoulders and held Amerie's gaze. "What's that supposed to mean?"

Instead of answering, she studied my face for several minutes. I kept my mask in place and stared back as hard as I could. Amerie slid her eyes toward Rilynn and then moved her attention back to me. "None of us want to hurt kids…"

"What are you trying to say, Amerie?" I growled.

She held her hands up and sighed. "You have Beth. What are you going to do when you're faced against a child that reminds you of your niece?"

Beth's smiling face flashed in my mind.

Don't think or feel, Greer

Forcing Beth's image from my mind, I put as much authority in my voice as I could. "I am willing to do whatever it takes to keep my sisters and any other member of the military safe." I breathed deeply and held Amerie's gaze. "I know my ROEs. I know my job. If there is an immediate threat, I will take it out."

Amerie leaned her shoulder against the wall and watched me for several heartbeats. Neither of us said anything.

Slowly, she nodded. "Alright, then."

I gave a curt nod and looked back at Valerie and Ziana. Their lips were tipped up as they chuckled at something Rilynn had said, but even from a distance, I noticed the shadows under their eyes and the tightness in their mouths.

The past two months had changed them.

My mind flashed with images of the small children we had passed last night sleeping in the ramshackle homes. Some of them were soldiers…perhaps all of them.

Sighing, I ran a hand through my hair.

For the first time, I wasn't thrilled to be back at work.

Chapter 9

"Hell yeah!" Dee cheered as we jogged down the street. "This is so much better than the coat of shame."

I glanced back quickly and smiled. "Nice to be able to see."

Dust billowed around us and I breathed in the smell of cordite and smoke. Adrenaline hummed within my body as I paused in front of a doorway. Behind me, I could hear the labored breaths of the small unit of Marines we'd been assigned to.

Dee stepped forward and locked eyes with me.

I gave a curt nod.

The door crashed open, and I rushed inside with my finger hovering over the trigger as I quickly scanned the area.

Silence greeted me as I entered the living area of the small home. Pounding footsteps echoed down the hall as the Marines checked the rest of the house.

"Clear in the front," I stated.

Dee strolled next to me, holding her M4 down by her side. "This is the fifth empty home in a row we've infiltrated."

Hearing the uneasiness in her tone, I turned toward her. "Yeah, I know."

According to the Marines and SEAL Team Two, none of these houses were ever empty. A firefight always happened, that's why it had been taking so long to take back Damascus. So why was it so easy today?

A knot settled in my stomach. Something wasn't right.

Dee kicked at some torn rugs. "I don't like this."

Wiping the sweat from my brow, I nodded. "I don't either."

Footsteps approached from behind us, and I whipped around to see a tall, lanky Marine.

"All clear. No signs of any intel."

I nodded. "Thanks, Jones." I started walking out the door. "Let's move out."

Off in the distance, I could hear spurts of gunfire. I glanced up and noticed billows of smoke coming from the east.

Bookie…

I took a quick look at the block of houses we had left to check. My hands twitched, and I forced myself to take a deep breath. I wanted to go help my teammates and be in the action, not stuck with the vacant homes.

"Radio's been quiet," Dee mumbled next to me.

Not making me feel better, Sheba.

"Yeah."

I scanned the area around us. Goosebumps chilled my skin. Pausing, I looked around.

"You feel that?" I whispered.

Dee nodded.

My finger stayed close to the trigger as I opened up my senses. I took a step forward, my gun raised. All of a sudden, a body fell above me. Darting to the side, I dodged the falling body just before it crashed on top of me.

"Holy shit!" Jones shouted. "What was that?"

My head swiveled toward a tall building several hundred yards away. "Cutting it a little close, Legacy."

Chuckling filled my ears. "He wasn't anywhere near any of you."

I rolled my eyes. Behind me, Dee snorted.

"Overhead is pretty badass," Jones commented.

I turned back and scoffed. "Don't let her hear you say that." At Jones's scrunched eyebrows, I gave him a little smirk. "Her head is already big enough."

"Heard that." Amerie said, annoyed.

Turning back around, my smirk grew. "Wasn't trying to hide it."

We made it to the end of the street to the last house. Dee met my gaze as we stopped in front of the door. I gave a slight nod and tightened my hold on my gun.

Dee barged the door open and I dashed in with my M4, ready to fire. Shrill screams immediately filled the small space.

"Get down!" I yelled.

I pointed my gun at three women in burqas and five small children. Tears ran down the youngest child's face. My stomach churned seeing his small, tearful face. He had the same curly hair as Beth.

Shaking my head, I kept my gun positioned on the women while the others swept the rest of the house. Cordite, sweat, and smoke mixed in with the strange spices coming from the kitchen.

One of the women stared defiantly at me with a cold, hard gaze through the mesh square as I checked her for weapons.

I had no doubt this woman wished me dead. I could see and feel the hatred coming off of her.

The little boy rushed to the woman, and she wrapped her arms around him, speaking softly. I could just make out the woman telling the boy to remember his duty. Worry and anger rushed through me as I recalled Rilynn's warning from yesterday.

"Check out this crazy shit."

Out of the corner of my eye, I saw Dee and Jones shoulder past the Marines keeping watch to stand next to me. Making sure to keep the woman in my view, I glanced from my peripheral vision and noticed an RPG in Dee's hands.

"Where is everybody?" I asked in harsh Arabic.

The woman stared back with narrowed eyes but remained speechless.

I took a step toward her, causing the little boy to start whimpering louder. "Stronghold like this, why were you left so unprotected?"

Something didn't sit right with me.

I pointed to the Marines carrying out weapons. "A stash this big would not be left unguarded with a bunch of *women and children*." I spat my words out at the woman. "Where. Is. Everybody?"

"I've got heavy movement barreling toward you, Kid," Legacy said over the comms. "Three technicals and about sixty to seventy tangos."

The woman let out a small laugh, chilling my skin. Dee caught my eye for a second and then quickly made her way to the door.

My gaze wandered over the thin walls and then toward the dead end street. We were trapped.

I narrowed my gaze at the woman and shouted at one of the Marines to take the other women and children to another room out of the way.

"Legacy, how far out?"

The rumbling of vehicles shook the building.

"About a klick, maybe two."

Grabbing Jones and a handful of other Marines, I pushed them toward the stairs. "Head to the roof and take them out from there. I'll help take them from the ground." Jones gave me a quick nod and rushed from the room with four others.

I took the woman roughly by the arm and shoved her into the room with the rest of her group. "Better hope the bullets don't make it this far." I tucked the kid behind the woman and then stationed a Marine by the door.

Gripping my weapon, I glanced out the doorway and saw Dee and three Marines crouched behind a half-crumbled wall. Making sure the other Marines in the house had bulletproofed their positions as much as possible, I darted out into the street and eased in next to Dee.

"Legacy?"

Before she could answer me, a technical raced around the corner, spraying bullets. Dust and gravel kicked up around me as I returned fire. Overhead, Jones and the other Marines quickly joined the fight.

The technical continued to speed toward us.

"Oh my God!" a young Marine shouted next to me. He slumped down the wall, covering his head with his hands.

I took another shot at the driver before glancing down at the young man. The way he covered his head, I couldn't tell if he was hit or not.

A bullet whizzed by my head, causing chips of concrete to cut into my exposed skin.

"Damn it," I hissed.

The sticky feeling of blood caused my loose hair to cling to my forehead. I lined my sights up and tried to hit the driver that was still speeding toward us.

Dee's shoulder bumped into mine as she fired rounds at the driver. "Check him out. I got this," she yelled.

Crouching low, I tried to push the man's hands away. "Let me see."

Wide eyes stared back at me.

I sucked in a breath.

Even under the helmet, I recognized the blond hair. The man's legs bounced just like they did the first time I saw him on the plane going to induction.

"It's you," he whispered.

I nodded and quickly scanned his body, searching for wounds. "Yup. Thought you avoided the draft," I snipped.

He balked. "Didn't make it to the courthouse with her…" He wrung his hands. "She married someone else."

I scowled.

Damn coward.

"Get up," I said harshly as I shoved his gun back into his hands. "There's nothing wrong with you."

He shook his head. "I can't…I…"

I shoved his shoulder hard into the wall. "Man up and grow a pair!"

His mouth parted in shock.

"You sit here and do nothing, we're all dead. You want to live?"

He blinked a few times and then slowly nodded.

"Then fight."

He swallowed as sweat trailed down his face, looking like a lone tear. His wide eyes darted around and then stilled.

Without looking, I knew he had found the small alley off to the side.

The coward was going to run.

My gaze flicked down to the name on his uniform before I glared at him. "Don't even think about it, Bowe," I growled.

"Hurry, Kid," Dee yelled. "We could really use some help."

I glared at Bowe. I wasn't going to waste another second on him if he didn't decide to man up soon.

He gave a small shake of his head and some of the desperation to flee left his eyes.

Good choice.

I roughly pulled him up and helped position him to safely shoot. "Just take out as many as you can."

He fired, and I quickly lined someone else in my sights. The street was littered with radical men. Out of the corner of my eye, I saw a Marine fall to the ground near the house's doorway.

"Man down!" I yelled.

"Air support and a convoy are on the way," Legacy stated as someone dragged the fallen Marine back into the house.

Next to me, Dee lifted one of the RPGs and took aim at an approaching technical. Heat from the blast brushed against my sweat-covered face.

"Damn." I turned my head away from the flames.

"I don't think they appreciated me using their toys," Dee shouted as she started firing with her M4 again.

I took some more shots as the other radicals started tossing their homemade bombs at us.

"Nope, I don't think so," I yelled over the falling gravel and gunfire. Next to me, Bowe started to whimper, causing my eyes to roll.

A loud roar started to rumble above us. The sound grew and then the Brits came flying over, spraying the rest of the radicals with a torrent of bullets.

I looked up and smiled. "Hell yeah."

Dee laughed. "The Brits still know how to send a message."

The one remaining technical flew in reverse and quickly left the street. I fired at the remaining foot soldiers and slowly lowered my gun. Dust and debris settled over the area like a blanket of fog.

I scanned the street, searching for any leftover threats.

An eerie silence greeted me.

Dee nudged my shoulder. "Good work."

I gave her a side glance. "You too."

My gaze shifted from her to Bowe. Dirt and sweat covered his face and body. Feeling my stare, his wide eyes met mine.

Dee glanced from me to him and frowned. "I thought he was hit."

"Nope."

Hearing the sting in my tone, Dee raised an eyebrow. Ignoring her question, I took a step toward the injured Marine, but she pulled me back.

"I caught bits and pieces on the radio when the Brits flew over, it doesn't sound severe." She eyed Bowe up and down with a scowl. "I know enough to keep him stable till we exfil. If it's a severe wound, I'll call for help, but you need to handle *this* before we leave."

Bowe hung his head low and shuffled his feet. I nearly rolled my eyes again. Dee spared one last glance at Bowe and then headed toward the others.

Feeling the anger within me start to boil, I had to take several breaths before I could look at Bowe.

You can't shoot him, you can't shoot him, you can't shoot him…

I repeated that over and over until I started to believe my mantra. Feeling back in control, I slowly turned toward Bowe. He held my gaze for a second and then his eyes quickly darted back to the ground. The feeling of déjà vu washed over me.

"First fight?" I asked more calmly than I felt.

Bowe's eyebrows nearly touched his hairline.

Don't worry, buddy, just because I'm not yelling doesn't mean I'm not pissed.

He took a deep breath and nodded. "Yeah." He wiped his hand across his brow and let out an almost hysterical snort. "I wasn't expecting it to be so crazy."

I scowled at him. "Get used to it." Ignoring his pale skin, I continued, "This is Damascus. What happened today is going to be your new normal." I took a step toward him. "If you want to make it home alive, you won't hide and cower while others put their lives in danger."

Bowe looked dangerously close to either wetting his pants or fainting. The sight of his fear pissed me off even more.

Grabbing a handful of his shirt, I got in his face. "If you *ever* even think about running off again, I will make sure you spend the rest of your life in prison." I shoved him toward the road directly across from the injured Marine. "Because someone else pays the price for your cowardice."

Bowe's face lost all trace of color. "Is he…?"

I glanced at Dee standing above the young man. She grabbed some gauze from her med bag and placed it against the man's shoulder.

I breathed a sigh of relief when she didn't call for my assistance. Turning toward Bowe, I shook my head. "He looks like he'll make it, but he's very lucky. Next time, that might not be the case. Do you understand?"

Bowe licked his lips and slowly nodded. "It won't happen again," he whispered.

"It better not."

A low roar of approaching vehicles echoed down the street. Bowe clutched his gun and quickly raised it toward the approaching convoy.

I shoved his arm down. "Relax. That's our ride out of here."

Red tinted his pale cheeks.

Scowling, I nodded toward his group of Marines. "Go wait with them."

He hesitated a moment before walking away. I spared his back one last glower and then made my way toward Dee.

"Damn snowflakes," Amerie growled in my ear. "Things got pretty loud, but did I hear you tell him to grow a pair?"

My lips tipped up. "Maybe."

"Atta girl!" Amerie cheered proudly, causing me to chuckle.

Dee looked up with a smile as I reached her.

She waved a hand over the injured young man. "How'd I do?"

Squatting down, I peered at the man's blood-soaked shoulder. "Not bad." She had stopped the bleeding, and done everything she could for him out here.

I smiled at the young man. "Our guys will be here soon, and we'll get you properly fixed up."

Standing up, I looked at his wound once more before spotting Bowe standing a few feet from the group I told him to wait with.

This whole situation was screwed up—an ambush, an attempted desertion, and a wounded Marine.

The convoy pulled to a stop. Several men jumped out and scanned the area. I turned my head and held my breath as a wall of dust crashed down on me. Movement from the house grabbed my attention.

I turned to see several Marines escorting the women and children from the home. The youngest child's tears had stopped, and he now shared the same cold expression as his mother. His gaze met mine for a second and then he abruptly turned his head.

"What do you think is going to happen to them?" Dee asked.

I shrugged. "The women will be interrogated. I'm not sure about the children."

As soon as the words left my mouth, the little boy darted away from the Marines and raced toward the wall at the end of the alleyway.

"Where's he going? There's nothing there." Dee asked as two Marines darted after the child.

A cold feeling washed over my skin as Rilynn's warning once again filled my ears.

As soon as the thought popped into my head, the little boy reached down behind a small wall of rubble and pulled out a small satchel. The boy clutched it to his chest and started racing toward the approaching Marines, his black curls bouncing.

Images of Beth flashed through my mind.

Panic swelled inside of me.

"Stop!" I yelled. When the boy continued to run, I yelled for him to stop again in Arabic.

The little boy's feet slowed, and he glanced at me.

My heartbeat pounded in my ears as I slowly raised my hands. "Stop. Don't do this," I ordered in Arabic.

The boy paused, his eyebrows pulled together.

In my peripheral vision, I saw the Marines that had chased the boy had ducked behind a pile of rubble. Seeing them safely away from the child, I felt myself breathe easier.

"It's over. Set the bag down," I commanded the boy.

He looked at the bag, then me. Just as he appeared to be lowering the bag, the boy's mother yelled at him to remember his duty.

Dread filled me.

The boy's head snapped up and the hatred returned in his eyes. He raised his little hand holding the detonator and began to run toward the Marines again.

Instead of an explosion, a single gunshot rang out.

The boy crumpled to the ground. I watched his dark curls bounce over his lifeless body. Bile filled my mouth and I had to really focus to keep from vomiting.

Briefly closing my eyes, I turned my head and walked back toward Dee. My eyes slid over her face just long enough to see the sickened expression she wore.

A lump formed in my throat and I had to swallow several times before I could push it away.

God, please watch over the child.

Dee cleared her throat and walked over toward me. "Now what?"

I glanced at her and then at the waiting convoy. Shouldering my gun, I walked toward the front Humvee.

"We go back to work," I mumbled.

"CLEARED ANOTHER INFESTED NEST," Emersyn announced.

Wiping the sweat from my brow, I pushed air from my lips, trying to generate a small breeze.

Amerie plopped down next to me in the Humvee. She rolled her head back and forth, popping her neck.

"Long seven days…" I huffed.

Amerie nodded. Out of the corner of my eye, I saw the haunted look that had been in her eyes since the day she had taken out the little boy.

Dee glanced at the two of us. "What do you think this

meeting with T.R. is about?" she asked, expertly changing the subject.

Emersyn popped her knuckles. "Probably a new mission."

I looked at her and grinned mischievously. "Bookie, you're such an Einstein."

Emersyn scowled at me, while the others laughed. Even Amerie seemed to gain some of her usual sparkle back.

We walked into the small office and found T.R. sitting behind a desk. My gaze wandered over a worn four-by-six picture frame sitting in the middle of his desk. T.R.'s little girl and his wife smiled broadly up at us.

T.R. cleared his throat. "We don't have any time, so I will get straight to the point. A new team will be replacing you tonight."

I felt my back straighten, and I glanced at the others out of the corner of my eye. Each of my sisters wore similarly perplexed expressions.

Reading the questions in our eyes, T.R. shook his head. "You're needed somewhere else more important."

My first thought was Russia, and then Africa. There had been a lot of chatter regarding the movement in those areas. Several attacks had been made in the past weeks, and our troops and allies were losing ground.

T.R. met my gaze. "New York."

I felt my eyebrows rise to my hairline. *America?*

Once again, T.R. answered our unspoken questions. "Riots have broken out all over the country. America is close to breaking out into civil war."

My stomach churned. This was not good.

"You exfil in twenty minutes."

The four of us nodded in response.

T.R. gave a curt nod just as his phone started ringing. He glanced down at it and sighed. His gaze met ours as he reached for it. "You girls did good work. Continue doing that hard work at home."

We walked out and silently made our way down the hallway. We had just reached our rooms when Amerie shook her head.

"Never thought we'd be having a mission in our own country."

Chapter 10

THE COOL WIND BIT AT MY SKIN AS I MINGLED WITH THE crowds. I shoved my hands deep into my pockets and scanned the area around me.

"Damn. Never thought I'd say it, but I kind of miss Damascus," Amerie said, teeth chattering. She leaned against a telephone pole with her hands wrapped around a warm mug of hot chocolate. Warm steam rose up around her face.

"I prefer Texas," I quipped as I walked further down the street. A deep yearning filled my stomach as I thought of home. "Same weather, sometimes warmer, but no one is shooting at ya."

"Yeah, yeah," Amerie mumbled. "There's no place like Texas."

A huge smile popped onto my frozen face. "Ain't bragging if it's true."

Off in the distance, I heard the familiar shouting of curses and derogatory comments. Scowling, I pushed my feet faster.

"Remind me why we're undercover," Dee grumbled.

"Because there is already too much violence and the president cannot afford any more negative media attention regarding the military and the people," Emersyn drawled. "If he sends in a SEAL team on his own people, can you imagine what the Lame, Fake Stream Media would say?"

I snickered. "I love when sassy Bookie comes out to play."

"I doubt President Macleod cares what the news stations say about him." Amerie took a sip of her hot chocolate. "The man is willing to do what it takes to get the job done. I respect that."

"You just like that he has no filter like you."

Three snorts filled my ear as I reached my destination. Standing at the top of some stairs, I surveyed the incoming crowds.

I glowered at the sight. "Keep your eyes and ears open," I ordered. "Stop the violence before it starts."

I watched as Dee started walking toward a group of Black Lives Matter protestors. Behind her, Emersyn made her way toward the Antifa group, while Amerie slid in with the Alt-Right. Once everyone was in position, I joined the antiwar protestors.

A group of police officers stood behind barricades. Each group was divided into their own little section, but the treaty between peace and violence hung by a thin, weak string. Just one rebel and the whole system would fall.

As if some unspoken command had been given, the Antifa group started brandishing their signs and shouting as loud as they could at the Alt-Right. In response, the Alt-Right started doing the same. Before I knew it, every group began yelling, cursing, and waving their arms around.

"And let the shit show begin," Amerie grumbled.

For a moment, I could only stare with my mouth open. The first image that popped into my head was a two-year-old throwing a temper tantrum for not getting their way. My eyes narrowed to slits, and I crossed my arms as I watched the scene before me. This was ridiculous. There would be no solutions. No one was listening. No one was accomplishing anything. The only thing I saw being done was severe damage to everyone's vocal chords. And across the world, people were dying to keep these assholes free.

A woman shoved past me yelling about her right to freedom of speech and how no one would take that away from her. My eyes drifted down to her bulging belly. She looked as if she could go into labor at any second.

I fisted my hands and walked away from her. "No one is taking away your amendments, you hippie idiot," I mumbled.

I waded through the tide of angry, deprived protestors, searching for targets wanting to take their protesting to the next level.

A man around my age took a step toward the barricade. Suspicion pulled me toward him. Using my small size, I weaved and wormed my way through the crowd until I stood next to him.

"Our war is not overseas. Hatred is here!" the man shouted. "Violence is not the answer." He reached into the inside of his coat pocket and wrapped his hand around a water bottle filled with yellow liquid.

The distinct smell of urine hit my nostrils.

I scrunched up my nose as the man started to unscrew the cap.

Just as the man prepared to throw the bottle at the line of police officers, I stumbled into him.

The bottle flew from his hands and crashed down at our feet, splashing urine all over the man's legs and mine.

The things I do for my country…

Dark brown eyes glared down at me. "Watch it!"

"Sorry," I said softly. Holding up my hands, I tried to keep the anger from my eyes.

The man looked me over with a frown. Some of the anger left his eyes, and I noticed an appreciative glint.

Resisting the urge to roll my eyes, I lightly placed my arm

on the man's forearm. "I'm so clumsy." I giggled and then tossed my head to the back of the protestor's line. "I've got some more stocked up." I let my lips curve up into a suggestive smile. "Want to come help me stock up with supplies to throw at these hate-driven Nazis?"

The man glanced from me to where I tilted my head. I waited as he threw another curse at the line of guards.

"Let's go teach these pigs a lesson," he said, grabbing my wrist and pulling me through the crowd.

I let him lead me away until we reached the edge of the crowd. Flipping my wrist around, I grabbed a hold of his arm and tugged him toward the right.

"I parked over here," I threw over my shoulder.

The man looked down at me and then over my head for my waiting car. "Which one is yours?" he asked as he matched his stride to mine.

I gave him a side glance and gave him my first genuine smile of the day. "It's just around this corner."

He rounded the bend in front of us and abruptly stopped. "What the hell?"

The man's mouth dropped as he stared at a small group of National Guard officers and a handful of handcuffed individuals.

Before he could utter a sound, I grabbed the man's wrists and pinned them behind him. "You are under arrest for attempting to incite a riot." The man started to argue with me, but I continued to read him his rights.

When I finished, I set him down next to a woman whose baby daughter slept soundlessly beside her feet. The small, rickety car seat holding the child made my stomach churn.

This woman didn't deserve to be a parent. Like a coward, she brought this child into the world to avoid the draft, and now, selfishly endangered her just to protest and express her beliefs.

My clenched fists started to shake as chants from the protestors fueled my disgust. The majority of these people shouldn't be here. They should be at home, working to provide for their unborn children, or taking care of their young babies, not jeopardizing their welfare. I had never seen such lack of parenting.

"Selfish cowards," I muttered under my breath.

The woman spit at me. "You dirty pig!"

Gritting my teeth, I glared at her. I started to turn away when she tried to kick me. Sidestepping her pathetic attempt, I got in the woman's face. "Don't even think about it."

Fear ignited in her eyes but quickly transformed back to anger.

I leaned back and snorted. "You don't know how lucky you are."

Her mouth dropped. "Are you threatening me?"

I shook my head. "You live in a country that allows you to talk shit about it. If you lived anywhere else, they'd arrest you, or worse, kill you for the things you are saying and doing." I took a step toward the woman and held her gaze. "Like I said, you don't know how lucky you are."

Before she could utter a sound, I spun around and stormed away.

"And I put my life in danger to protect ignorant imbeciles like you who don't give a damn about my sacrifices," I mumbled.

Scowling, I shook my head.

God bless the USA.

Clenching my fists, I made my way back to the protestors. The yelling seemed even louder now. I scanned over the angry mob, feeling the agitation in the air.

"Status?" I called out.

"Three a-holes locked up over here," Emersyn answered. Her tone and saint mouth made some of my anger slip away.

"Two racists are off the streets," Amerie chimed in. She let out a long groan. "Ah, come on…"

I looked over Amerie's section, searching for her.

"Some loser asshole just threw a water balloon filled with pink paint at me," she griped. "Bookie, you'd better arrest that little shit. This jacket cost me several hundred dollars."

I scoffed. "Well, at least it wasn't urine."

"Ugh…" Dee blurted. "You're not sitting next to me on the ride home."

"Oh, shut it, Sheba." Despite my harsh tone, I couldn't help but smile. "How are things in your section?

"I've arrested two who were about to start throwing rocks or some other crap." Her breathing filled my ears as she walked past a group of people howling. "People are starting to get more agitated."

Dee was right. All of the groups were becoming more daring with their attempts to disrupt the peaceful gathering.

"Just keep taking out the instigators," I ordered as I weaved my way back through the crowd.

Out of the corner of my eye, I noticed one of the under-cover agents escorting a protestor away. "We keep rounding up the leaders and we should be good."

Across from me, a tall woman marched her way toward the front of the protest line. Around her waist were bottles filled with red and pink paint. Groaning, I pushed my way toward her.

Just as I reached her side, a loud rumbling filled my ears.

I glanced up at the sky where it sounded as if a raging hornet's nest buzzed above. The hostile mob's shouts slowly trickled out as every head turned up to the sky.

I reached for my weapon.

"Kid, we weren't told anything about a fly-over, were we?" Amerie asked.

My stomach dropped at the suspicious tone in her voice. "No."

Next to me, a woman with a megaphone in her hands gaped as she stared at the sky.

I quickly grabbed the amplifier and ran to the line of police officers. "Everyone, find cover!" I yelled. "We are under attack!"

As soon as the words left my mouth, a plane zoomed overhead. My eyes narrowed on the North Korean flag that dominated the side of the plane.

For a heartbeat, the plane just flew over, but then it began spraying bullets at the protestors. Screams filled the air as people frantically scrambled to get out of the line of fire.

"Get everyone to safety!" I yelled into my radio.

Running in a zigzag motion, I started grabbing and pushing people into covered alleyways and into building as more and more planes joined the siege.

A woman around my age screamed loudly as a bullet tore through her leg. Without thinking, I raced toward the woman and lifted her up.

Her agonized wail pierced my eardrum as I sprinted to a pizza parlor.

"I'm hit…I'm hit," she whimpered.

"Shhh," I soothed. "You'll be fine." Easing her into one of the booths, I tugged off the black bandana she wore around her neck and applied pressure to her wound.

I glanced up and watched in horror as people sprinting for their lives were shot down like targets. The snow turned into a riverbed of red as bodies fell to the ground.

For a heartbeat, I watched as an Antifa protestor fell face

first next to an Alt-Right protestor. My mind drifted back to history lessons about the Civil War and how brother fought against brother.

I shook my head.

"Together we stand. Divided we fall."

Chapter 11

Screams continued to fill my ears.

Darting out of the building, I rushed forward to grab another wounded protestor. A young man clutched at several holes in his stomach. His hands were drenched in blood.

"Am I going to die?" the man stuttered.

Overhead, several planes continued their path, flying farther into the city, but a few circled back for another round. Grabbing the man's shoulders, I pulled him away as fast as I could from the incoming bullets.

He yelled out in pain as I dragged him across the snow.

"We need someone to start taking out those planes!" I shouted into my radio.

"Working on it," Emersyn answered, breathing heavily.

Across the street, Amerie and Dee rushed down the sidewalk, dragging the wounded to safety before the next attack hit.

"I'm so cold…"

I glanced down at the young man in my arms. His eyes began to droop and his breathing became shallow.

"Hold on," I said, my voice strained as I tugged the man. "We're almost there."

The buzz of the planes' engines became louder and louder. Snow and pavement started shooting up as bullets tore toward us.

The glass doors to the pizza parlor came into view. Digging deep within myself, I picked up my speed.

"Open the door!" I yelled at a group of bystanders watching.

The whizzing bullets flirted around the man's feet as I dove back into the parlor. Glass rained down on us as the plane passed.

Screams of terror and pain erupted around us. A sharp stinging pain sliced through my arm. Hissing, I glanced down at the trail of blood dripping down my arm.

"Oh my God. Are you shot?" a woman shrieked.

"No." I pulled out the shard of glass protruding from my arm. Glancing down at the man below me, I looked over his wounds.

I rocked back on my heels and sighed.

Blood dribbled down his chin as his wide eyes stared at me. "Am I going to die?" The man started choking on his blood, and I raised his head to keep him from drowning in the red liquid.

I smiled warmly at the man. "No. You're going to be just fine."

I took his hand and gave it a gentle squeeze. Next to me, a blonde waitress stood with round eyes. Waving her over, I placed the man's hand in hers. "Stay with him," I ordered.

"What do I do?" she asked.

The man's breathing had become irregular. Sighing, I closed my eyes briefly before meeting her gaze. "Just make him as comfortable as possible." Tears filled the waitress's eyes. "Talk to him," I added gently.

Rising to my feet, I rushed toward the door again. Before I left the restaurant, I noticed a group of uninjured protestors huddled behind the bar. Spinning around, I marched toward them.

"All of you, let's go. I need help moving the wounded to safety."

They glanced between one another, but no one moved.

I gritted my teeth. "Now!" I growled. "We don't have any time to waste. Those wounded in the street are easy targets for those planes to pick off."

A young woman with peace symbols painted on her pale cheeks stood up and scowled. "We'll be killed if we go out there. This is all the military's fault. If they hadn't entered World War III, none of this would have happened."

Next to her, the Antifa member with a black bandana hanging around his neck stood up. "Yeah, and I'm not risking my life to save some racist Nazi."

"Same," the woman protestor from the Black Lives Matter group announced. Blood dripped from a gash in her forehead. "They've killed enough of my people."

The tall, lanky Alt-Right man stood and clenched his fists as he glared at the other protestors. "Y'all sorry pieces of—"

"Enough!" I growled.

All four protestors jumped and stared at me with wide eyes.

"I don't give a shit about what you believe in." I took a step toward them. "You are all Americans. You are all the same." I stared each of them in the eye, letting them see the anger, disappointment, and utter disgust of my fellow countrymen in my eyes. "Each of you thinks you are a part of something that matters. You think you are making a difference." I waved a hand toward the wounded slowly dying in the street. "If you really want to stand for something that matters, help your fellow countrymen...help your country."

I looked into each of their eyes, hoping they'd put aside their differences long enough to see we needed to work together.

Tortured cries drifted into the restaurant.

When none of them moved, I shook my head in disgust and turned toward the door. Just as I reached the threshold, a hand grabbed my arm.

I looked back and saw the young woman from the Black Lives Matter group. "What do we do?"

Behind her, the others stood with their arms crossed, waiting for my instructions. I gave them a small nod and then checked for any approaching planes.

"Grab as many wounded and get them to safety before another wave comes."

Seeing clear skies, I rushed back out onto the scarlet street. The first set of bodies I met stared lifelessly back at me.

A choked sob came from the war protestor.

I glanced back at her and frowned. "We have to find the wounded. I know it's tough, but keep moving."

"How are you so calm?" she sobbed.

Ignoring her, I jogged toward a young woman crawling on her knees, holding a blood-soaked hand to her stomach. Gently, I rolled her onto her back and pushed her hand out of the way.

"Shhh, everything's going to be okay," I soothed as I pulled out the gauze I had thankfully stuffed in my pockets as a precaution. Quickly, I covered the woman's wound and ordered her to keep pressure on the bandage.

"How do you know how to do that?" hippie woman asked again.

When I didn't answer, she covered her hands with her mouth. "Oh my God, you're one of them…you caused this."

Wrapping an arm around the injured woman's waist, I eased her up onto her feet before I met the war protestor's stare. "In case you didn't notice, those planes had North

Korean flags on them. Last I checked, North Korea hadn't joined this World War, and we weren't fighting them."

My breath came out in ragged puffs as I half-carried, half-dragged the wounded woman to safety. "Looks like being peaceful with them didn't stop them from attacking." I gave the war protestor my "don't argue with me" glare. "Go get the wounded. Another wave can happen at any second."

I made my way as quickly as I could toward a small office building. Someone held the door open as I dragged the injured woman inside. Passing her off to someone else, I started back for the street.

Just as I walked out the door, Amerie walked in.

"Legacy." I breathed a sigh of relief. Amerie's face was covered in dried and fresh blood. Her gaze swept over me as she checked me for any injuries.

"I'm fine." I waved my hand over her. "What about you?"

She handed off a wounded man and nodded. "I'm good."

A small smile flitted onto my lips. "And Bookie and Sheba?"

"We're good, too," Dee answered over the radio.

I closed my eyes and said a little prayer of thanks.

"Fighter jets are on their way," Emersyn informed us. "Apparently, there's a top secret landing field close by."

I passed by an overturned, burning police car and bent down to check the pulse of a girl who barely looked fifteen. Feeling nothing, I closed her eyes.

The loud rumbling of an approaching aircraft sounded again. Screams of terror filled the streets as the protestors raced for cover.

"Bookie, are those friendlies?" I called out.

"Negative," she answered.

Damn it.

Standing out in the middle of the street, I scanned for

wounded still needing help. My gaze danced over the motion-less bodies, searching for one I could help. I ran down the rows of people until I saw one twitch.

"Help me," a teenage boy rasped.

His bloody hands clutched his stomach, where a massive gash covered his lower torso. A scarlet-covered street sign leaned against his leg.

Careful to avoid any more damage, I eased my arms around the boy's waist and helped him stand up. He cried out in pain as we started hobbling toward the nearest building.

The sound of the approaching aircraft became a deafening roar. Sweat clung to my forehead as I tried to move faster.

The boy yelped as I helped him step over a dead body. He crumbled to his knees, and his heavy weight pulled me down with him.

"Come on, kid, I need some help."

The boy had tears streaming down his face as I struggled to move him again.

The roar of the engines rattled the windows.

Above us, five planes swept back toward the street, firing a relentless barrage of bullets. Tearing away from the incoming threat, I glanced toward the awaiting building several yards away.

We're not going to make it.

Breathing deeply, I pushed the boy to the ground and covered his body with two dead protestors. Snow and gravel kicked at me as the bullets flew closer and closer to where I stood.

Satisfied with the boy's safety, I grabbed the nearest body and threw it on top of me just as the whizzing buzz descended down on me. Snow and broken chips of pavement flew as bullets sprayed all around us. Warm liquid coated my skin and dripped into my mouth.

Coughing, I turned my head and prayed my plan had worked.

As soon as the buzzing started to drift away, I shoved the dead body off of me and watched as the five planes merged with the rest of the fleet flying toward the ocean.

"Kid!" Amerie's wide eyes met mine as she sprinted toward me. She reached my side and grabbed my shoulders. "Are you okay? Are you hit?"

I shook my head. "I'm fine."

I wiped the blood from my face and went to go help the boy, but Dee and Emersyn were already there.

Amerie looked down at the bullet-riddled corpses that had protected the boy and me and shook her head. "I thought you were a goner."

So did I.

Before I could answer, a few planes broke away from the group and circled around the Statue of Liberty, taking turns spraying her with bullets.

My hands fisted, and I took a step forward.

"Oh, hell no!" Amerie bellowed. She looked around, desperately searching for some kind of weapon. Seeing nothing, she let out an aggravated yell. "I feel so useless." She turned toward Bookie. "Where the hell are those fighters?"

As if they heard her, the fighter jets zoomed past us. Their turbulence nearly brought me to my knees as they raced toward the retreating North Korean planes.

For a moment, none of us said anything, we barely breathed. Around us, people started trickling out of their hiding places and searching for the wounded again.

I watched as people forgot their differences of opinion and beliefs and started helping one another. The division lines were no longer drawn. For the first time in a really long time, we all worked together; we were united.

I gazed out through the smoke toward the sea. Off in the distance, I noticed a small orange glow surrounding Lady Liberty.

Even from this distance, she looked angry. I could see parts of her were chipped and broken, but she still stood.

And she was pissed.

Chapter 12

"WHAT THE HELL DO YOU MEAN YOU HAD KNOWLEDGE OF AN imminent attack?"

My eyes widened as I watched Senior glare at CIA Director Bryan James on the projector screen. I had never heard Senior raise his voice like that and, honestly, I was more than a little frightened.

Director James's lips formed a thin line. "We were not certain the information was credible."

"I'd say the hundreds of civilians shot dead in the streets provides enough proof the information was pretty damn credible."

Director James broke eye contact and glanced down at his hands.

"What exactly was the intel?" Senior growled.

Director James swallowed thickly before meeting Senior's gaze. "One of our agents had concerns someone had the ability to hack our alert systems, preventing us from seeing approaching aircraft until it was too late to intervene. We didn't think it was plausible." He whispered the last sentence so low I had to strain my ears to catch it.

Senior cursed under his breath and shook his head. Next to me, Amerie crossed her arms and glared at the projector screen.

"Damn idiots," she mumbled.

"I want to speak to this agent," Senior demanded.

The director opened and closed his mouth a few times before finally giving a small nod. Rising like a recently disciplined child, he moved out of the camera's view. I could hear chairs scraping the ground and papers being shuffled before a middle-aged man with a receding hairline took the director's seat.

My jaw dropped. Next to me, my sisters sat up straighter in their seats.

Dark shadows loomed under Nolan's eyes. His hair looked longer and more disheveled than how he usually kept it. My gaze drifted to his CIA badge that held a picture of him before the Damascus incident.

I felt a pang of sadness as I looked at the happier, more naïve Nolan. The man on the screen no longer resembled the man in the small picture. This new man knew the ugliness of war, and he knew how it felt to bury a good friend.

My throat constricted.

Nolan's gaze flickered over us before moving to Senior. He gave a slight nod. "Senior."

"Mr. Gaines." Senior's voice became less clipped and more like his usual tone. "You knew something like this was going to happen. How?"

Nolan frowned. "For the past few months, our alert systems would glitch and malfunction for a few minutes." A muscle twitched in his cheek as his eyes hardened. "It looked like a technical malfunction, but I had seen something similar during my time in Damascus."

Images of blank monitors flashed through my mind. I could still see the beads of sweat trickling across Nolan's forehead and hear the fear in his voice when we learned we had been compromised.

Nolan cleared his throat before continuing. "I became suspicious our alert systems were being hacked, so I started doing some digging." His hands tightened around the folder he held. "What I found did not warrant enough proof of intel to state if the hack came from a foreign country or some harmless kid."

Even though nothing about this situation was funny, I couldn't help but smirk at Nolan's dig at the director. From the corner of my eye, I saw Amerie's nod of approval.

"During the attack this morning, I learned how they hacked our system." Nolan leaned forward, and a dangerous glint appeared in his eyes. "I can do the same thing to them. I know how to hack their system to find the aircraft carrier they've hidden from radar. What they did to us, we can do to them before they make it back to their country."

Adrenaline hummed through my body.

I glanced at Senior and saw him nodding his head. "This will have to be a decision for the president. I'll start calling my superiors." He picked up the phone and began dialing. "You start working out the plan for Operation Retribution."

He glanced up and locked eyes with Nolan. "Let's make these assholes pay."

MY GAZE TRAVELED from the screen to the blood still staining my clothes and hands. Images from yesterday's attack flashed through my mind.

Blood-soaked streets, agonized screams, bright flames surrounding the Statue of Liberty...

"You look like you could use this."

The scent of fresh coffee washed over me. Breathing in the enticing aroma, I took a sip of the rejuvenating liquid. "Thanks, Sheba."

She nodded. "I can't believe you drink that stuff black."

She eyed me like a volatile creature from another planet, causing a small laugh to escape my lips.

"I know what I like."

She shook her head as she took her seat next to me. At the end of the table stood Senior, his arms crossed. Nolan sat beside him, furiously typing away on his laptop. Nearby, several different monitors showed a live feed on the projector screen.

"Think this will work?" Amerie whispered.

Keeping my eyes on the screens, I whispered back, "It has to."

Emersyn leaned forward, sitting on the edge of her chair. "They're about five klicks out."

My legs bounced under the table. Taking a deep breath, I watched as a large aircraft carrier came into view. At the end of the ship, a tall North Korean flag danced in the wind.

My hands fisted, and I took another breath.

"This will work. It has to," Amerie chanted so softly I barely heard her.

On the screens, the jets quickly moved into fighting positions. The ship looked asleep. No one on it seemed to be aware of the approaching danger.

Hope began to bloom in my chest. This was going to work.

I watched as the fighters paved the way for the bomber. A blaring alarm rang out and the people on the ship began scurrying around, racing to mount a defense.

I heard the command and then watched as several bombs slowly descended toward the aircraft carrier, leisurely falling from the sky. My heartbeat slowed, matching the bombs' pace.

I held my breath as they connected with the ship.

For a heartbeat, nothing happened, and then a huge wall

of orange and yellow exploded into the sky, forming a bright sphere around the center of the ship. Like dominoes, the planes began to explode as more bombs were dropped. A few people scrambled on the deck, but their movements were futile. Within minutes the entire ship was swallowed by the ocean.

Leaning back in my seat, I breathed a sigh of relief.

Applause and cheers erupted in the small room. I glanced at Nolan and saw him release a deep exhale. I doubted he had taken a breath since the mission started.

Scooting my chair back, I walked over to Nolan and clapped him on the back. "Good work." I gave him a quick wink. "By the way, super proud of that sassy dig yesterday."

His eyes gained some of the light I remembered as he smiled at me.

"Yeah, not bad." Amerie patted his shoulder. "Where did an interpreter learn all of that computer hacking stuff anyway?"

Nolan chuckled. "I was always more than just an inter-preter." The light in his eyes dimmed a little as a frown drifted onto his face. "But Angelette taught me a lot."

He cleared his throat and ran a hand through his messy hair. He glared at the screen. "I'll make sure our systems are never hacked again."

Before any of us could reply, the TV in the corner of the room blared with a special update. President Macleod sitting behind his desk flashed onto the screen.

Amerie glanced at me and raised an eyebrow. "This ought to be interesting."

Nodding, I walked closer to the television.

President Macleod stared directly into the camera. "The New Year is about new beginnings. The opportunity for a better you, a better life. For six hundred and twenty-one

Americans, their 2024 ended before it had even begun." President Macleod's voice lowered to a cold tone. "North Korea made a deliberate, callous attack on American soil." His lips formed a thin, tight line. "They viewed us as weak...divided..." he leaned slightly forward, "...but they failed to remember that during turmoil, we Americans *stand together*. We. Do. Not. Back. Down."

Goosebumps chilled my skin.

"Yesterday, I watched courageous acts of heroism as individuals risked their lives to save those who did not share their ideals and beliefs, *racing* into the line of fire to save their brothers and their sisters. Because like any other *family*, we Americans have our disagreements, but when push comes to shove, we have each other's backs. We. Fight. For. One. Another."

President Macleod paused for several heartbeats before continuing. "When our family is harmed and our home is threatened, we band together and we crucify those who had the gall to wrong our family." He folded his hands across the top of his desk. "The year 2024 is America's new beginning. We *will* be respected by our allies. We *will* be feared by our enemies. We *will* fight to protect our home."

The screen held his determined gaze for several seconds before switching back to the regular news.

Amerie let out a low whistle. "That was some call to arms speech."

Dee nodded. "It made me want to fight."

I glanced over my shoulder at Senior talking on the phone in a hushed voice.

"But will it make others want to fight?" I asked as I turned back to my sisters. "It's like Bookie said, we need more people to join this war, we can't be everywhere at once."

Before anyone could say anything, Senior ended his conversation and called us over to him. He folded his arms and looked over each of us. "President Macleod wants to send a clear message to North Korea. He wants to strike their heart."

From the corner of my eye, I saw both Emersyn and Dee listening intently with blank expressions. Amerie, on the other hand, wore a wicked grin. She tilted her head just enough in my direction to give me a quick wink.

I felt my lips twitch.

Nothing ever bothers that girl.

Senior took the time to hold each of our gazes.

"This mission is voluntary." He paused, giving us the option to back out. When none of us moved, he gave a nod of approval. "Exfil in twenty. You'll learn the details of the mission on the way there." He turned toward Nolan. "We're going to need you to hack the system again."

A wicked glint appeared in Nolan's eyes. "It'd be my honor."

Senior's lips tipped up into a small smile before he addressed us again. "Go pack. Make your call home and do whatever else you need to do to get ready."

Without another word, he walked from the room. I turned to Nolan and smiled. "See you in a few."

He gave me a quick smile before moving toward his laptop.

Amerie walked over to my side. "Another secret mission…"

I smirked at her tone. "Are you seriously keeping count of these kinds of missions so you can brag about it to your brothers one day?"

Instead of smiling, Amerie's mouth turned down. Tension and worry reflected in her eyes, and she quickly looked away.

I placed my hand on her shoulder. "What happened?"

She licked her lips but kept her gaze away from me. "Not sure, but my brothers haven't called home in a while."

My stomach knotted. "Maybe they're out on an op and haven't had the time to call."

"Yeah…" she nodded, running a hand through her hair, "…I'm sure that's it."

Hearing the doubt in her voice, I gave her a small smile. "They put up with your annoying ass, they'll be fine."

Amerie chuckled. "Hush it. You better go call your family while you still have the time."

Ducking away from her punch, I pulled out my phone, smiling. "Already on it."

Amerie was still laughing as I walked from the room with my phone to my ear. After a few rings, Brooke's voice popped up on the other end.

"Hello?"

"Hey, stranger."

"Greer!" Brooke exclaimed. "How are you? Where are you? Is everything okay?"

Laughing, I rolled my eyes. "Calm down. I'm fine. I'm at work." I shook my head and walked into my room to pack. "I should be asking you if everything is okay. Why are you answering Mom and Dad's home phone?"

Brooke let out a relieved sigh. "We had Beth's birthday party today…"

A sharp pain stabbed my chest.

I'm the worst aunt ever.

With everything going on, I had completely forgotten about Beth's birthday. A large lump found its way into my throat.

"Your mom and dad are out there watching her and her little friends play," Brooke continued as I focused on shoving the lump away. "You should have seen her blow out her candles on her cake. She looked just like Charles eating your dad's eggs."

A small laugh left my lips. I could picture Beth's cheeks filling up with air as she tried to blow the candles out in one breath.

"She is one very spoiled little girl. Your parents got her a fancy little coloring kit, and she's already told everyone how she plans to draw you pictures of everything you've been missing so you don't feel left out."

Tears pricked my eyes, and I had to sit down on my bed. I hated missing all of this.

"She got some cute little outfits, a Barbie Jeep, and some roller skates," Brooke rambled on. "She's out there driving her friends around right now. Let me go get her."

"No," I rushed out in a thick voice.

I heard Brooke's sharp inhale, and I quickly cleared my throat. "Don't bother her. I know she's having fun."

Brooke paused for several seconds before she answered. "Do you want me to get your parents or brother?"

I shook my head. "No, it's fine. I don't have much time to talk. Just tell them I love them."

Taking a deep breath, I grabbed my gear and headed out the door. On the other end of the phone, I heard Brooke walking through the house and then shutting a door.

"Is everything okay, Greer?" she asked softly.

"Yeah, everything's fine," I reassured her. "I just had some time to call and wanted to see how everyone was doing."

"You're leaving again, aren't you?"

I sighed. My best friend knew me too well.

"Where are you going?" she asked.

"You know I can't answer that."

She released a shaky breath. "You only say that when it's something dangerous."

"Well, we are in World War III," I teased lightly, hoping to draw away the worry in her voice.

"This isn't a joke, Greer," Brooke snapped harshly. She took a deep breath, and then said in a calmer tone, "North Korea attacked New York yesterday."

Trust me, I know.

"Things are getting bad out there," she added.

I ran a hand through my hair. "I know. I promise I'm being careful."

A small sob came from Brooke. "You'd better be. Because if you're not, your niece and nephew will not be happy with you."

"I'll be…" I stopped abruptly as Brooke's words trickled into my brain. "My nephew?"

My mouth hung open as Brooke let out a happy sob. "You're the first to know."

"Oh my…congrats," I stuttered out.

Brooke let out a sad chuckle. "So come home soon, okay. I need my best friend here."

"I'll do my best." I looked up to see the others loading up into our ride and sighed. "Hey, I hate to go, but we're about to head out."

I knew without seeing her that tears were streaming down her cheeks. "Okay," she said thickly. "You stay safe."

Smiling, I strolled toward the others. "I promise. Tell everyone I love them, and tell Beth happy birthday for me and that I'm sorry I missed her big day."

I ended the call and took a deep breath, forcing the lump out of my throat.

At times, it felt like the outside world didn't even exist, and then with just one little phone call, that illusion shattered.

Nothing constricted my heart more than hearing the big and small details I missed in my family's life.

I hated not being there with them, but my job allowed my sweet Beth and, soon, my nephew to have birthday parties and to have a normal life.

We will fight to protect our home.

President Macleod's speech filtered into my mind. My hands clenched as I recalled the orange and yellow flames surrounding the Statue of Liberty.

The need for retribution sparked within me.

North Korea messed with the wrong country.

Chapter 13

I SCOWLED AT THE WATER.

Why?

Lifting my eyes to the sky, I kept asking God the same question over and over again.

Why water? In the middle of winter?

The last thing I wanted to do was take a swim in the middle of the Yellow Sea, but God and Senior didn't seem to care what I wanted.

Next to me, Amerie snickered. "Keep staring at it, you may make it boil."

Unamused, I narrowed my eyes at her. "Shut up."

Amerie laughed and continued to get her gear ready for our lovely swim. "Ready to get your ass kicked?"

Ignoring Amerie, I tried to forget I could see my breath in front of my face. "The things I do for my country," I mumbled.

My gaze wandered over the rough waves and then traveled over my sisters. Emersyn sulked at the end of the small boat, grumbling under her breath, while Dee and Amerie sat by one another talking animatedly among themselves. Judging by the glints in their eyes and waving hands, they were talking trash to one another.

Crazy speedboats.

I rolled my eyes at the two of them. Tilting my head to the side, I locked eyes with Senior. He walked over and clasped his hands behind his back. "I got you as close to Pyongyang as I could."

Shaking my head, I rubbed my hands together. "I know."

Senior glanced back to where Nolan sat inside the tiny cabin of the rusty fishing boat. His fingers looked like they were running sprints over his laptop's keyboard.

"His new code should keep this boat hidden from any radars…"

"But we can't risk a Chinese fishing boat getting spotted close to the North Korean borders. I get it," I finished for Senior.

He chuckled. "Then stop moping around." He looked back at Emersyn and shook his head. "You two are SEALs, act like it."

I nodded. "Hooyah."

Off in the distance, I could just make out the outlines of another vessel in the early morning fog. I glanced down at my gear one last time before meeting Senior's gaze.

"Showtime."

He gave me a brief smile before turning to address the others that had gathered around us. "Make me proud."

I looked at each of my sisters as determination filled me. We'd get the job done.

A huge grin popped onto Amerie's face. "You got it, Pops."

Smirking, I met Senior's gaze. "Can't say she isn't persistent." I glimpsed his smile just as I dove into the water.

Sharp needles stabbed my body as I adjusted to the sudden change in temperature. My black wetsuit blocked out most of the chill, but the frigid water still found a way to sneak into my bones.

In front of me, Amerie led the group with a steady stride. Blocking out any discomforts, I forced my mind to empty.

Just pretend it's another swim in the Pacific, Greer…no big deal.

Even after all of the months since BUD/S, I could still recall the early swims we did each morning. A few times, the water had been colder than this.

I smirked to myself as Senior's voice floated into my mind. "It could always be worse."

I quickly found my rhythm and just swam. We took turns taking the lead, alternating every ten minutes to keep one person from exerting more than another. Our system reminded me of my high school athletic days, when my coach would have the entire team perform Indian runs for conditioning. As I swam behind Dee, I couldn't help but wish we were doing this on land.

"I am loving this lightweight rebreather," Amerie's awed voice disrupted my thoughts. "We'll have about forty minutes left of oxygen after this little fifty-minuet dip." Her voice transformed into a goading tone. "After we strike the heart of North Korea, what do you say we go for another swim? Bookie, Kid?"

Rolling my eyes, I ignored her taunt. In front of me, Dee's shoulders shook from her barely contained chuckles. She slowed her stride, letting me know it was my turn to lead.

Forcing my weary muscles to propel me through the water, I took my place in the front. From the corner of my eye, something flashed in and out of my vision, making my heart go into overdrive.

Twisting my head around, I glimpsed a dingy shoe dangling from a fisher's net. Its shoelaces wriggled and danced with the current. My muscles unclenched as I let out a shaky breath.

"Better watch them sneaky shoes," Amerie snickered.

Raising my middle finger, I kept pushing forward. I could

feel the smug grin plastered on Amerie's face, and it made my competitive spirit come rushing out. Clearing my mind, I forced my body to keep the pace Amerie had started. Every muscle in my body ached, but I ignored their protests. Unrelenting, my arms and legs propelled me forward. I didn't slow until my turn at the front came to an end.

Satisfied with my performance, I couldn't help but give Amerie my best sardonic look as she passed me to take the lead for the final stretch.

The challenging glint in her eyes promised I'd regret provoking her. Before I could dwell on my actions, I felt a gradual change in water temperature.

"We've reached Korea Bay," Emersyn cheered.

I smiled. "Getting closer to Taedong River."

Almost done.

Amerie twisted her head just enough for me to catch her malicious look and then she shot through the slightly warmer waters. Despite the faster speed, energy surged through my tired muscles. I could see the finish line.

About halfway during her turn, Amerie angled our course.

I took a quick look at my gauge and smiled. We only had a few minutes left in the water.

Controlling my breathing, I let the current push me forward. Amerie swam a couple more feet and then halted. Slowly, she raised her eyes just barely above the water.

Coming up from a different angle, I mirrored her movements. I scanned the area, searching for the slightest motion.

Complete silence fell over our small group.

"Clear," I whispered.

"Clear."

"Clear."

"Clear."

Amerie crept forward to the bank of the river with the rest

of us following behind her. My feet sank into the mud as we trekked through the riverbed. Rocks then shifted under my feet, followed by a floor of grass and pine needles. Silently we moved into the cover of the trees. We all crouched into position and scanned the area, searching for anything out of place.

No one breathed or twitched a muscle.

"Alright, Bookie, make the call," I whispered as I grabbed my waterproof case out of my pack, and took out my gun.

Emersyn pulled out her comms to let Senior know we had made it. She moved deeper into the cover of the trees but stopped when static came from her comms. Grumbling under her breath, she moved back to the riverbed.

My breath created a small cloud in front of my face as I waited under a tower of trees. A small rustling of leaves came from my right. I glanced at Emersyn and arched an eyebrow.

"Communication is going to be restricted to river valleys." Her lips curved up into a taunting smirk when she glanced at Amerie. "Senior said to have a nice little hike in the woods."

My own lips twitched.

Oh, Karma, you are so fair and just.

Emersyn's smirk grew. "The mountain ranges here are pretty severe, but that means we shouldn't have to worry about running into any settlers."

I nodded in response as I changed out of my diving gear. When everyone had their gear situated, we started trekking forward. As I passed Amerie, I made sure she saw the wicked glint in my eyes. "Hope you can keep up."

Other than an eye roll, she kept her thoughts to herself.

Frost covered the ground and the trees around us. A cool breeze whistled through the leaves, freezing the few loose strands of my hair to my cold cheeks. Setting a decent pace, I marched silently through the trees and brush.

After a few minutes, the tree lines started to thin a little, revealing the steep slope of a mountain. Rocks and boulders jutted out at an irregular pattern. I craned my neck back and sighed.

Here goes nothing.

Behind me, Amerie groaned.

No longer appreciating Karma's payback, I turned back and met Amerie's scowl. "Thank God for BUD/S."

Her lips twitched. "And Senior's ruthless training."

Heading up the slope, I nodded. If it hadn't been for all of that hard work during training, there was no way I would have had the stamina for this hike.

Rocks and gravel slid under my feet as the sun peeked over the early morning fog. The muscles in my thighs and calves quickly started to burn as the slope continued to rise. Ignoring the pain, I focused on my breathing and let my mind wander back to my family back home.

I started making lists of things to get for my little nephew: cowboy boots, onesies, his first little rope…

Images of teaching him to rope and ride the same way I taught Beth caused a smile to pop onto my face.

Dee strode up to take her turn at the lead. As she passed me, she cocked an eyebrow at me. "What are you smiling at?" she huffed.

I shrugged. "Just all of the things I plan to do when I get home."

She nodded. "Yeah, I'm thinking about all of the gumbo and crawfish I'm going to have my granny cook for me."

I laughed. "After hearing all about your granny's famous cooking, we better be invited."

Amerie rubbed at her stomach. "I've never been much of

a seafood person, but I think I'll have to give Granny's cooking a try."

Dee chuckled. "Just be ready for a party." She glanced back and smiled. "My family knows how to have a good time in NOLA." A mischievous glint appeared in her dark eyes. "Especially when we all head to Jolie Boudreaux's bar."

Amerie's lips curved up into a wicked grin. "I'm thinking we need to go there first thing when we're stateside."

Smiling, my breath started coming out in ragged puffs as the slope started to go up again. A small trickle of sweat oozed down my back.

Twisting around a narrow curve, Dee let out a small curse.

I stepped to the side and peered around the others' backs. A nearly vertical rock ledge loomed in front of us.

Dee looked up and then turned around to meet our gazes. "I'll go first."

I nodded. "Be careful."

Amerie shifted her feet back and forth as Dee slowly made her way up the slope. Rocks slid down back toward us. About halfway up, her paced slowed even more as she meticulously placed her hands and feet into footholds, and eased up to the ridge.

"This is going to suck," Amerie grumbled.

I glanced at the blaring sun that had moved to the middle of the sky.

"Well, after this, we should be close to our mark." I glanced at Dee's waving hand at the top. "Alright, Bookie, you're up."

Emersyn started up at a quicker pace than Dee. Even with all of her comms equipment, it didn't seem to hinder her too much. At about the same point as Dee, Emersyn expertly placed her hands in the same footholds, and quickly climbed the rest of the way.

Amerie shook her head. "Damn spider monkey."

I laughed. "Now you know how it feels when you turn into the human speedboat."

Amerie mumbled something under her breath.

Shaking my head, I pointed to the mini-mountain. "You're up, Legacy."

Sighing, Amerie sulked up to the gravel slope. My lips twitched as she slowly made her way up. Compared to Emersyn, Amerie's form maneuvering around the jagged boulders was comical.

Guess that's how I look when I'm swimming.

About a quarter of the way, Amerie slipped and nearly fell to her knees. Rocks tumbled down behind her as she found her footing. Nervously, I felt the need to search my surroundings. I doubted anyone would be out this far from civilization, but with as much noise as Amerie was making, I couldn't help but pull my gun out in front of me.

After several tense heartbeats, Amerie finally scrambled to the top. I didn't need to see her to know she was spewing a list of cuss words my mama would have spanked me for.

Chuckling, I started making my way up the tricky slope. Starting out, I felt good, but that feeling quickly vanished. Rocks under my feet shifted, causing me to slip. Grumbling under my breath, I pushed forward, ignoring the fire burning in my thighs.

"Holy shit," I puffed as I gaped at the wall in front of me.

Giving my tired arms a quick shake, I let out a deep exhale before reaching up for the first foothold. The muscles in my shoulders and back strained as I heaved my weighed-down body up the wall. Using my core strength, I propelled upward as quickly as I could. Over my labored breathing, I could just barely hear Dee and Amerie softly speaking. A small smile flitted onto my lips.

Ignoring the burn in my muscles, I pushed myself over the last big boulder. Dee's hand reached my sweaty one.

"Good job," she greeted before smirking down at me. "I think Bookie made it up faster though."

I glared at her. "Shut up, Sheba."

She laughed at my panting and tilted her head toward Emersyn. "She can't get a hold of anyone on comms."

I frowned and glanced around. "We're pretty high up. You'd think we'd get a signal up here."

Dee shrugged. "Only place it's worked so far was down by the river."

Easing back to my feet, I nodded. "Good thing that's our next stop."

I took a quick drink of water while glancing at the late afternoon sun. "Ready?" I asked.

Emersyn popped to her feet and took the lead. I waited for Amerie to fall in line before I started walking behind her. The ground remained flat for several strides and then began to gradual slope downwards. I glanced ahead and noticed several narrow twists leading back to the dense trees.

The sun began to droop low into the sky when we made it to the tree line.

"Finally," Amerie huffed.

Back in the front, I chuckled. "About two klicks left, Legacy." Keeping my back to her, I added, "Stop flipping me off."

Chuckles filled my ears.

Smiling, I crouched forward. I scanned the area, looking for anything hidden among the trees. We were still pretty far out from any of the settlements, but we could never be too careful.

The rush of the river drifted to my ears. Slinking through the trees, I kept moving until I found a thick bush to blend into. I pulled my gun around and scoped the area while Emersyn got her comms up.

Rustling to my right caused my muscles to tense.

Swiveling toward the sound, I gazed in the direction it had come from. Silence surrounded me, followed by another hushed rustle.

I moved my finger above my trigger and waited.

A heartbeat passed before I felt my lips slowly curve up as a familiar voice taunted, "They're not here yet."

Scooting from my hiding place, I beamed at the two Brits strolling through the trees.

"Hey, boys," I leaned against a tree and smiled at Jasper and Sterling. "Long time, no see."

Chapter 14

STERLING BUMPED HIS SHOULDER AGAINST JASPER'S. "Pay up."

I arched an eyebrow at Jasper's scowl. "What was the bet?"

Sterling smirked. "I said you'd get here on time, he thought it'd be nightfall."

My lower lip jutted out in a mock pout. "I can't believe you doubted us, J."

He frowned and narrowed his eyes at Sterling, causing a snicker to escape my lips. "Legacy really corrupted you." I shook my head. "The J I first met wouldn't have even considered participating in such a devilish game."

I opened my arms to him. He shook his head and gave me a hug. "How's your wife?"

Jasper's eyes shone brightly as his face lit up. "About ready to pop." For a second, his eyes clouded with sadness, but he quickly pushed it away. "She should have him any week now."

The muscles around my mouth ached from smiling so hard. "That's great."

My gaze shifted to Sterling, who held his arms wide open.

"You staying out of trouble, Joker?" I teased as I gave him a quick hug.

His lips curved up into his special Sterling smile. "You tell anyone else to man up and grow a pair?"

Scoffing, I shoved him hard in the shoulder. Chuckles filled our little group. I listened and laughed at the jokes Amerie and Sterling passed around. For a moment, I forgot we were trespassing in a foreign country.

Too soon, our little family reunion came to an end and reality returned.

I glanced around the frost-covered forest. "Where are Doc and Hollywood?"

Jasper cleared his throat and transformed into the all-business man I remembered so well. "They're keeping watch at our base for the night." He tilted his head back. "It's just a few klicks."

I looked over his shoulder. At first, all I could see were trees, but then I noticed a gradual slope to the ground. Next to me, Amerie let out a sigh.

I bumped her with my shoulder. "Ready, Legacy?"

She narrowed her eyes at me. "I *never* want to hear you complain again when we have to travel by water."

I chuckled. "Deal." I started walking and then glanced back to give her a wicked grin. "At least we are above ground." I turned back around before she could utter a retort, but felt the burn from the middle finger she waved at my back.

Sterling matched my pace and laughed. "I see some things haven't changed."

My lips curved up. "Nope." I scanned the area around us. "How long have you been here?"

Sterling stepped around a large boulder. "Got in last night." The slope became steeper and narrower, forcing me to walk behind him. "So far, it's just been rocks and trees and these bloody mountains."

I snickered at his tone. "You sound like Legacy."

A loud huff drifted up to me. Smirking, I glanced over my shoulder and caught Amerie's annoyed glare.

"What all do you know about this mission?" Sterling asked.

"Not much." Frowning, I stepped over a fallen tree limb and recalled the information Senior had provided while we flew. "Just meet with one of our assets, gather intel from them, and then use that to take out North Korea's heart."

My breathing began to pick up again as the slope became steeper. "Oh, and that our asset can only make contact once, sometimes twice a month." The ground flattened back out, so I eased back up next to Sterling. "That quota's been met for the month." I smiled humorlessly at his frown. "Which means we can't contact our transport when we make it to Pyongyang."

Sterling nodded. "So you know as much as we do." He let out a breathless chuckle. "They can never make the mission too bloody easy for us."

Laughing, I caught Jasper's smirk as he took his turn in the lead. A sharp wind sliced at my frozen cheeks. Scowling, I lowered my head. "I hope they have some damn good intel." I rubbed my hands together, trying to create some warmth. "The quicker we find our mystery target, the quicker we can get out of here."

Sterling's eyes lit up with humor. "It's not that bad."

I gave him a sideways glance. "I miss my Texas weather," I grumbled.

The sun's rays dipped below the mountain ranges when he finally eased toward a low valley that backed into the side of the mountain. He dropped his gear by a tree trunk and waved an arm around the small area. "We'll camp here for the night."

I glanced around, looking for Evan and Parker.

Amerie strolled up next to me and gave an appreciative whistle. "Not bad, guys. Almost didn't see you there."

My forehead wrinkled as I strained my eyes in the direction she looked. Leaning forward, my gaze traveled over every branch, rock, and shrub.

I saw nothing.

Sighing, I asked, "Where are they?"

Amerie pointed her finger at an unsuspecting bush. "Hollywood." She swiveled to the right and nodded toward a set of boulders. "Doc."

The two men crept out. Evan wore a wide grin while Parker scowled.

"How'd you see them?"

Amerie turned toward me and smirked. "Uh…I'm the best." She rolled her eyes. "How many times do I have to tell you that?"

Jasper walked past us with a smile, shaking his head. Evan and Parker left their hiding places and walked toward us.

Evan smirked triumphantly at Parker. "I won."

Parker glowered at him. "Yeah, yeah, I'll pay you back later."

Evan wrapped a big arm around me.

"Hey, Doc." I returned his hug and then hooked my thumb toward Parker. "Do I want to know the bet?"

Evan grinned mischievously. "He didn't think you girls could spot us; I knew better."

Amerie punched Parker in the shoulder. "Never doubt my skills."

Parker rubbed his shoulder and smirked. "Noted."

Chuckling, I set my gear down and took a seat on one of the boulders. The frost seeped into my pants, but my weary, frozen muscles barely noticed. Breathing deeply, I looked around our little camp.

The side of the mountain provided a great north wind block, while the dense trees and brush made it easy to blend in. If anyone happened to be this far out in the woods, they wouldn't notice us. We had the perfect spot.

Dee took a seat next to me and released a weary breath. "Home sweet home."

The muscles in my mouth twitched at her tone. "Very spacious."

Dee shook her head and glanced around. Her gaze landed on Emersyn leaning against a tree and then moved to Amerie having an animated conversation with Sterling and Parker.

She narrowed her eyes at the campsite. "Do you think there are any, like, spiders or snakes around here?"

I reached into my pack and took out a granola bar. After taking a big bite, I shrugged. "We are in the woods…"

Her wide eyes met mine. Unable to keep a straight face, a small snicker escaped my lips.

Dee glared at me. "That's not funny."

Wriggling my eyebrows at her, I finished the rest of my granola bar and stretched. "I thought it was."

Dee pursed her lips and glowered. "I hate camping."

"Suck it up, buttercup." Chuckling at her glare, my gaze moved from her to Jasper across from me. He glanced up and met my stare.

I elbowed Dee and tilted my head toward him. "Come on." The hushed chatter around us ceased as everyone circled around Jasper.

He spread out a map against a large rock and then moved his finger diagonally across the page until he stopped on a small dot. "This is our extraction point." He glanced around, meeting all of our gazes. "All communication will be down." He frowned at the dot. "But transport has been prepped for our arrival. Our timing has to be perfect."

Parker folded his arms. "So, if we get there too early, we'll be sitting in the bloody open, and if we're too late, we get left behind?"

Jasper nodded. "Exactly."

Low mumbles filled my ears as I scanned over the map. "The hike will be about three klicks..." I glanced at the mountain ridge across from us. Even this far away in the growing dark, I could see the steep incline. "That mountain alone will take at least an hour, maybe two."

I looked at my teammates. Sterling met my gaze and winked. Shaking my head at him, I rolled my eyes. Nothing bothered him.

Jasper folded the map and nodded at my sisters and me. "Get some rest. We'll leave in a few hours." He turned toward Evan. "Take first watch."

As I walked away to make my makeshift bed, my mind swirled with all of the possible scenarios we'd run into tomorrow. Nervous energy twisted my stomach.

Tingles ran down my spine as a nagging suspicion settled deep in my gut. This wasn't our first challenging op, but never before had I felt so blind, so on edge. Something about this just didn't sit right with me.

Exhaustion pulled at my eyelids. Keeping my M4 tucked close to me, I closed my eyes and tried to ignore the incessant voice inside my head telling me we had accepted a Hail Mary mission.

Gazing across the vast river, I tried to slow my labored

breaths. Just through the dense fog hovering over the murky water, I could glimpse the edges of Pyongyang.

Behind me, Amerie sucked in a lungful of air. "We got up way too early to climb Mount Everest."

I glanced over the dark green river water and glowered. It was still too early to swim across an "ocean."

Instead of voicing my thoughts, I tilted my head toward her and arched an eyebrow. "You're seriously *that* out of breath from our little stroll through the hills?" I scoffed. "Someone needs to do more cardio."

Amerie scowled. "We'll see what kind of tune you're singing after our little dip in the pool."

Touché.

Next to me, Sterling laughed. "Still better than the telly." He finished pulling on his gear and then turned to me. "Things have been seriously dull without you Americans."

"I'm thinking we need to bring them home with us," Parker said, "England could use some of their spice."

"My wife would love to meet my little sisters." Evan wrapped an arm around Dee's shoulders as he beamed down at me.

"So would your brother," Parker teased.

Evan scowled at him. "I'd make sure John was on his best behavior."

Parker and Sterling let out deep chortles, causing Evan's scowl to deepen.

Shaking my head at the three of them, I finished tugging on the rest of my gear. Behind me, soft whispers drifted to my ear.

Turning, I caught Jasper talking to Emersyn. Despite the frost-covered ground, sweat dotted his furrowed brow. Tension knotted his neck and shoulders.

This mission bothered him more than it did me.

Feeling my stare, he lifted his head and caught my eye. Emersyn said something to him and he gave a resigned nod before walking toward me.

"Remember, all radios and electronics need to be turned off," Jasper stated for what felt like the millionth time. "The slightest frequency wave and this op is blown."

I met his gaze and gave a mock salute. "Got it, J."

My tone did its job. I watched as a small smile flitted onto his lips. Shaking his head, Jasper looked down at his watch. "Transport should be at the extraction point in ten minutes."

My stomach tightened as I looked at the vast river again. "We'd better get to moving if we want to catch our ride."

Wordlessly, we eased into the frigid water. Arctic daggers sliced through my suit as I slowly submerged my body. My teeth clenched together.

It could always be worse...it could always be worse...it could always be worse...

While I chanted my mantra, Amerie caught my eye. Her lips curved up into a wicked grin just before she vanished under the green water.

The glint in her eyes made my weary muscles cringe. Pursing my lips, I followed behind her.

Setting a relentless pace, Amerie darted through the water like a fish on steroids. I quickly forgot about the cold and focused solely on keeping her in view. Around me, the others propelled swiftly forward.

The river's current pushed me along, helping me swim faster than I ever had before. The water glided through my fingers and over my body. My legs burned from the exertion, but I kept pushing forward.

Sucking in a large gulp of air, I noticed Amerie's stride gradually slow as the edge of the riverbank came into view.

She floated in place and glanced over at Jasper. He looked down at his watch and gave a thumbs-up.

A dense layer of fog encircled our bodies like a fortified shield. Through the thick haze, I could just glimpse the blurry red image of a taillight parked by the edge of the river.

"Target in sight," I whispered.

Prowling a few strides forward, I eased up to the metal building next to the idling truck. The smell of fish floated on the wind, causing my nose to wrinkle.

The scent became stronger as the sound of shuffling feet disturbed the quiet morning. I melted into the shadows and barely breathed as an elderly man with a hunched back carried a basket full of fish. He hobbled past the building to the back of the truck.

Keeping the elderly man in my peripheral vision, I tilted my head just enough to catch Emersyn's eye. She gave a slight nod, and I let out a relieved breath. Emersyn puckered her lips and released a short, bird-like whistle. The man stepped into the truck, oblivious to her signal.

I gave her a side glance. "Maybe he's hard of hearing?" I mouthed.

Before she could reply, the man stepped out of the truck and walked back to the building. He returned a few seconds later with another basket of fish. This time as he walked by, he hummed a soft melody.

Emersyn gave another nod before she left the safety of the shadows and stepped toward the man. He gave her a toothy grin and held a finger to lips. He stepped into the back of the truck and waved us in.

Nodding, we all stepped inside. The man set the basket of fish next to several other baskets and then lifted up a wooden floorboard. Emersyn hesitated for a heartbeat and then eased herself down into the false bottom floor.

As Parker and then Dee followed behind her, my eyes darted to Amerie. The muscles around my mouth twitched as she glowered at the shrinking space.

Her gaze slid to mine. "Not a damn word," she mouthed.

Biting the inside of my cheek, I turned quickly to keep from laughing out loud. The man's eyes crinkled around the edges. He waved Amerie and me forward.

"Hurry, hurry," he whispered.

Nodding, I tucked myself close into Sterling's side. Amerie followed right behind me, and the man quickly positioned the floorboard over our bodies.

Darkness wrapped around us.

I couldn't wriggle an inch; I could barely breathe. We were packed in tighter than a herd of wild horses trying to rush out an open gate.

The truck rumbled to life and lurched roughly forward.

Partially on top of me, I felt Amerie's rigid body tense even more. "How well do we trust this guy?" she hissed through clenched teeth.

The thought had crossed my mind, but hearing the unease and distrust in Amerie's tone caused my stomach to churn. I peeked through the crook of her arm and looked through a pinky-sized crack. Blurry images of a gravel road flashed by. For all we knew, the old man could be leading us to our deaths.

The longer Amerie's question went unanswered, the tenser her body became. Flicking my gaze from the crack, I met her wide eyes. "Senior wouldn't have sent us here if he suspected anything."

My voice thankfully came out a lot calmer than I felt, and her body lost some of its stiffness. The truck rumbled over several potholes before easing to a stop. I peeked through the small crack and saw black boots illuminated by the red glow of a taillight.

I sucked in a breath. This wasn't good.

"What?" Amerie whispered.

I briefly met her gaze. "You don't want to know."

The sound of a car door creaking open echoed through our fish tomb.

Male voices spoke in hushed tones.

Purposeful footsteps marched across the gravel.

A pair of dark boots paused next to my crack.

I stopped breathing.

A bushy tail flashed by, followed by a wet black nose pressing against the crack.

Chapter 15

WARM AIR BRUSHED AGAINST MY FACE.

Frozen, I stared, wide-eyed, at the black nostrils.

Don't breathe…don't move…you're not here…

My mind kept chanting those seven words over and over until a speck of light trickled through the crack. Still paralyzed, I watched as the German Shepard eased backward. He twisted his head toward his handler and wagged his bushy tail. Together, they stood in front of the crack for one drawn-out heartbeat and then inched out of view.

A soft exhale left my lips.

Shrill barking erupted into the early morning air. The dog's warning bounced around our fish tomb. Running and shouting mixed in with the alarm.

I looked around our cramped space, searching for a way out. I couldn't reach any of my weapons, but maybe if there was another way out we could—

Whatever plan I was starting to make died when I caught Amerie's gaze. Her eyes held a resigned yet resolved glint. It felt like a punch to the gut.

We were trapped.

Instead of fear, a calm acceptance cascaded through me.

Recognizing the same determined glint in my eyes, a wicked grin curled Amerie's lips. She arched an eyebrow at me just before her gaze flicked down to her leg.

Straining my eyes, I could just make out the shape of a

raised rectangle. Understanding her meaning, my own evil smile emerged.

Silently, I stretched my arm as far as I could until my fingertips brushed against Amerie's SIG-Sauer 9mm pistol. Sweat trickled down my neck as I tried to grab it again.

Nothing.

Needing more room, I pushed my body against Sterling's stomach, knocking the breath out of him. His soft grunt tickled my ear just as the gun's warm handle molded against my clammy palm. Grasping it tightly, I yanked it free.

Outside, the shouting had softened, leaving only low grunts and groans of pain. From the corner of my eye, I could see the old man's grimy mud boots.

He talked softly with a young guard, their friendly tone suggesting the two knew each other well. My stomach churned as I remembered Amerie's earlier question. I guess he couldn't be trusted.

The old man and the guard shuffled out of view. I strained my neck, attempting to keep them in sight, when boots stomped above us.

Next to me, Amerie's gaze darted up to the shadow standing on top of our board. Silently, I shifted the SIG toward him and waited.

The guard moved around, leisurely pushing fish baskets across the floor. After a few seconds, he said something to the old man and jumped off.

My heart slowly began to beat again as I heard the old man open and close the creaky door.

The truck crawled forward.

Loosening my chokehold on the SIG, I released a shaky breath.

Thank you, God.

As we passed through the concrete barricade, I caught

sight of two small children, handcuffed. Tears flowed down their tiny faces as they stared at their beaten, motionless parents.

Bile filled my mouth.

The image of the parents' broken and bloody bodies stayed with me as the truck ambled down the gravel road. Taking a deep breath, I pushed their faces from my mind and focused on watching the blurry landscape.

We traveled over the bumpy road for several minutes before I felt a slight slope to the ground. Wheezing and whining mixed in with the truck's rumbles as it slowly crawled over a hill.

"That'd be our luck..." Amerie groaned. "Stupid truck croaks, keeping us trapped in this fish casket."

Chuckling, I closed my eyes and absorbed the heat from the soft yellow rays peeking through the small crack. "Don't jinx us, Legacy."

The truck coasted down the hill and then rounded a corner before pulling to a stop. My gaze briefly met Amerie's before drifting to the floorboards above us where the old man shuffled around.

His low grunt vibrated our tomb as he lifted a basket and walked away. A few minutes later, the truck rumbled back to life and eased down the street before stopping about a block away. Once again, the old man hobbled onto the back of the truck and left with a basket.

After the twenty-second stop, Amerie groaned. "Is he going to keep us stuck in this damn casket all day?"

My lips twitched.

Emersyn's whispered, "He only has a few more baskets left."

Amerie rolled her eyes. "She would know that," she mouthed.

A silent chuckle shook my shoulders, shooting sharp knives into my arms and legs that had long ago lost circulation. Grimacing, I turned back to my peephole. The sun shone brightly on small, grey homes. People scurried down the sidewalks and streets, hurrying to complete their morning tasks.

I tried to memorize every street sign and building I glimpsed. I had no idea what road the old man's intel would lead us down, but I wanted to be as prepared as possible when the time came for us to travel it.

The truck made three more stops and then pulled into a tin garage. Smirking, I gave Amerie a pointed look. "As usual, Bookie's right again," I whispered softly.

Amerie rolled her eyes. "Yeah, yeah," she mumbled.

The truck's rumbles vibrated our tomb as it slowly backed into the small building. A door creaked open, and the same soft melody from earlier drifted over me. Rattling chains mixed in with the humming and then a metal door slammed shut.

Darkness rushed in, temporarily blinding me.

Shuffled footsteps slowly hobbled across the floor.

Amerie moaned. "Can he be any slower?"

Resisting the urge to taunt her, I watched the floorboards above me wriggle back and forth. After several tugs, one finally budged free, and a burst of fresh air rushed over my face. I inhaled a deep, greedy breath.

Air, sweet fresh air...I'll never take you for granted again.

Still humming the melody, the old man held a finger to his lips and waved a hand at us to hurry out. Sterling let out a small groan as I pushed into him to give Amerie some space to move. A grimace flashed across her face as she crawled from the fish tomb. The moment her body cleared the floorboards, I moved to follow her.

A thousand knives stabbed and sliced my oxygen

deprived limbs. Air whooshed out of my clenched teeth as I gingerly eased out. Massaging my arms, I took in the space. Wooden crates lined the tin wall and fishnets hung from the ceiling. Lingering in the far corner, a bucket filled with different sized fishing poles claimed the rest of the small room.

Once everyone filed out of the truck, the old man replaced the floorboards and then ushered us through a side door. We quickly passed through a mudroom into a small living room. A single couch and bookcase filled the space. Across from the couch loomed an old TV.

The man walked up to the bookcase and pushed it a few feet to the side. He bent down and removed several floorboards. Amerie's shoulders sagged as she let out a low groan. Glowering at the wooden ladder concealed by shadows, I resisted the urge to do the same.

Still humming the melody, the old man pointed at the ladder.

A small sigh left my lips.

He didn't offer any type of explanation, he just expected us to get in the black hole.

The silent treatment put me on edge. The old man may have gotten us safely into the capital, but I still wasn't sold on trusting him. Maybe if I had a name or something, I'd feel a little more comfortable about the situation.

I looked down to the dark hole and then back up to the old man. Before I could open my mouth, he quickly shook his head and placed a finger to his lips. He glanced over his shoulder while waving a hand at the ladder.

"Hurry, hurry…" he whispered. "Not safe. Talk later."

Jasper frowned but made his way down into the hidden room. The old man began nodding in encouragement as the rest of us followed.

Stepping off the last rung, it took my eyes several seconds to adjust to the darkness. Nothing filled the small room except a few rugs and pillows that covered the concrete floor.

"Looks like we got the Ritz again," Dee whispered as we shuffled to the far corner.

"Good to be back…" I couldn't help but snort as I recalled the last time I told her that.

Shaking her head, Dee stared at one of the pillows and grimaced. Trying not to laugh at her discomfort, I watched Parker climb down the ladder and into the hidden room. His feet hadn't even touched the last rung when the floorboards snapped back into place. A loud scraping sound came from above, and then nothing.

Blinding darkness and a deafening silence surrounded us. For several heartbeats, no one moved. No one spoke.

I stared at the ladder and frowned.

Emersyn sighed softly, her hand wrapped tightly around her Star of David necklace. She dropped onto a pillow and mumbled, "Guess this is how my ancestors felt…"

I stared at her small frame but remained mute. I had no idea what to say.

None of us did.

Giving in to my weary muscles, I eased down onto a pillow and leaned my head against the wall.

Plopping down beside me, Jasper ran a hand through his hair. "Everyone, rest up." He propped a pillow behind his back and stretched out his long legs. "We may not get another chance for a while."

Chapter 16

Time crawled by.

Seconds felt like hours. Hours like days.

I rested off and on, but every hobbled footstep and whispered conversation jolted me awake. My ears would strain to hear more, but the sound always drifted away.

The heavy tension in the air pressed down on my constricted lungs. With each passing heartbeat, the apprehension in the small room grew, amplifying the unspoken question: how well could we trust this man?

Late in the evening, scraping sounded above. Silently, we all rose to our feet. Dust and dirt sprinkled on top of my head as my fingers inched toward the trigger of my M4.

A trickle of light rushed in, followed by a toothy grin.

"It safe now." The old man's smiling face backed away from the small hole, and I caught the slight huff as he struggled to stand back up.

Amerie and I locked eyes. She gave a slight shrug and bounded up the ladder.

My lips twitched at her eagerness.

Following behind Dee, I was one of the last to leave the hidden bunker. As soon as I stepped into the small living room, the beaming old man rushed forward to vigorously shake my hand.

"So good to meet you."

Jasper came up the ladder behind me, and the old man quickly moved to shake his hand.

"So good to meet you." The old man's gaze traveled over each of us, his toothy grin stretched broadly across his weathered face. "I wait long time to meet you…" He held up a finger. "America told me be ready. One whole year, I wait for you to come, and now, you in my home." He beamed at us. "I am honored."

My forehead wrinkled. A whole year?

Oblivious to my shocked expression, the old man continued to ramble on in choppy English. "My name Yang Yoon. Everyone call me Eobu…mean fisherman." He waved a hand toward the couch and a few kitchen chairs that now invaded the tiny space. "My home. Your home."

I nodded. "Thank you, Eobu…" When his name passed my lips, it came out sounding unsure and wrong in my dialect. Out of the corner of my eye, I noticed Amerie biting her lower lip, trying to stifle a snicker.

I'd like to see you do better…

Ignoring Amerie, I smiled at the old man. "We appreciate everything you have done for us."

Evan and Sterling nodded as they took a seat on the couch.

The scent of river water floated to my nose, reminding me of this morning. I tilted my head away from the smell and met Eobu's gaze. "Do you mind me asking? How'd you get us past that checkpoint?"

Eobu's eyes crinkled. "You smell like river and fish. Trick dog." His brown eyes clouded with sadness a frown appeared on his wrinkled face. "People try to leave North

Korea, not enter. My grandson say a family get caught every day."

Jasper arched an eyebrow. "Your grandson was there this morning?"

Eobu's frown deepened. "Have no choice. All men, sixteen to forty, must serve."

Before any of us could respond, the nearly antique television clicked on. I whipped my head toward the static-filled screen.

"What the...?" Amerie's hand rested on the handle of her holstered SIG as she stared, wide-eyed, at the screen. "Sheba, is that thing possessed?"

Dee cocked a hip and crossed her arms. "Is there a reason you think I'm the ghost expert of the group?"

Amerie edged behind the couch and scoffed. "You're the one who lives in a voodoo city..."

Chuckling, Eobu shook his head. "Funny girl." He chuckled again before easing down onto one of the wooden chairs he brought from the kitchen. "It time for nightly news."

"It just pops on like that?" Amerie asked as the static morphed into a slightly blurry picture of North Korea's leader.

Eobu nodded. "Not allowed television or internet." He nodded his head toward the TV. "Watch what he allow."

Clips of soldiers climbing into planes filled the screen. The planes weaved between crumbling buildings and broken skyscrapers. A male voice said a few words just before a city of shabby tents came into view. Screaming blared from the speakers as people dressed in threadbare rags scurried out, desperately trying to flee from the bullets. Applause and cheers sounded as the camera zoomed in on motionless bodies.

Out of the corner of my eye, I noticed Sterling's furrowed brow. Across from him, Emersyn glowered at the screen that now displayed images of the Statue of Liberty burning to the ground.

The same male voice spoke again and then the TV abruptly clicked off.

Emersyn shook her head. "Propaganda at its finest."

"You mean fake news," Amerie grumbled.

Emersyn turned toward Eobu. "What did they say at the end?"

Frowning, Eobu shifted in his seat before meeting Emersyn's gaze. "Death to America," he said quietly.

Jasper walked over and grabbed one of the kitchen chairs and placed it in front of him. "Sounds like we don't have a lot of time." Sitting down, Jasper leaned forward and placed his elbows on his knees, effectively putting him at Eobu's eye level. "Tell us everything you know."

Holding Jasper's gaze, Eobu folded his wrinkled, cracked hands in his lap. "We not allowed internet. We have no access." The corner of his lips tipped slightly up. "But out in boat, far from shore, I get small signal."

I walked around in front of the couch and took a seat next to Evan. "That's why you can only make contact a couple times a month."

Eobu nodded. "But now I must travel much farther." He pointed over his shoulder toward the kitchen. Above the stove, a small, dingy window revealed a storefront. "River fisherman say it much worse. Mess up good boat. Force to take boat from when he was little boy."

Emersyn frowned. "Some kind of signal interference?"

Eobu shrugged. "Large military trucks still work."

Jasper leaned back in his seat and pulled out the map from his back pocket. "Show me where."

Eobu leaned forward and dragged a finger across the page. "Once a month, they leave and go here. Not sure how far they go after here."

Jasper stared at the spot Eobu had pointed to for several seconds before arching an eyebrow. "Here?" he asked pointing to the spot again.

"Yes."

I leaned forward to get a better view of the map and frowned. "There's nothing out there."

Parker walked over to my side and glanced down. "Except rocks and trees and those bloody mountains." He looked at Eobu. "You positive?" He placed a finger on the map and then slid it across the page in the opposite direction. "Not this way?"

Eobu nodded. "Friend complain they scare all the fish away." He tapped the map with his finger. "You find tire tracks here."

Jasper's gaze lifted up to meet mine. "You think there's something out there?"

I looked down to Eobu's finger still on the map. Could the mountains be hiding North Korea's heart? I pursed my lips as I mulled over that possibility.

Made sense. It was where I'd hide something.

Slowly, I began to nod. "I think something unimportant wouldn't have been hidden somewhere so secluded from civilization." I glanced at Emersyn and saw her nodding in agreement. "I think, whatever it is, it means a lot to them."

Emersyn walked over and glanced down at the map. "They wouldn't waste an interference system that strong where no one lived."

Jasper gave a curt nod as he folded the map. "How soon can you get us out of here?"

"Before sun come up." Eobu's eyes crinkled as he grinned. "And before you lose river and fish smell."

Chuckling, I looked over my shoulder just in time to catch Dee's grimace.

Amerie bumped her shoulder. "Ready to go camping?"

Dee's lips turned down. "Ready to go back to our room for the night," she shot back.

I shook my head at their banter as I stood up to help Eobu put the chairs back in the kitchen. My eyes wandered over the small space before settling on Eobu's hunched back.

"Eobu…"

He shuffled around to meet my gaze.

"Don't take this the wrong way, but why are you helping us?"

A sad yet warm glint entered his eyes. "This my home. But it not a good place. Not for long time." Reaching into his pocket, he pulled out a wallet that had more wrinkles than him and gingerly removed a faded picture.

I glanced down at the creased image and gazed at two smiling children.

"I want better for them." Eobu patted my shoulder. "You help make their life better."

I gave him a small smile. "We'll do our best."

Chapter 17

THE TRUCK CRAWLED TO A STOP.

I peeked through my crack and saw the same young guard from the other day walk toward the driver's door. Korean mixed in with the truck's rumbles.

A bushy tail flashed by and then disappeared.

Next to me, Amerie tensed as more voices floated toward us. Someone laughed loudly, and then the truck slowly began to ease forwards.

Sterling released a pent-up breath, tickling the back of my neck. "I bloody hate that part."

Unable to nod my head, I gave a low, "Mmhmm."

The truck ambled down the rough gravel road and then pulled to a stop. Eobu hummed his melody as he hobbled onto the back of the truck. Slowly, he wriggled the floorboards back and forth.

My constricted lungs waited impatiently for the rush of fresh air. After several prolonged heartbeats, a cool breeze brushed against my face, and I greedily took a large gulp.

Holding a finger to his lips, Eobu grabbed a basket and disappeared into the heavy fog. A shiver ran down my spine as a frigid wind pushed against my body. Scanning the area, I melted into the shadows while the others crawled out of the fish tomb.

Eobu returned for another basket just as Emersyn hopped out. His gaze traveled over our small group and he placed a weathered hand to his chest. "Honored." He stepped forward and grasped each of our hands. "Be safe and good luck."

I squeezed his hand back and smiled at his warm gaze. "Thank you for everything." I glanced up to where the checkpoint loomed a few miles away. "You be careful."

He patted my shoulder and then waved toward the water. "Hurry." Grabbing another basket, he briefly held my gaze and began humming again.

I watched the fog engulf his hunched form, and then silently followed the others to the edge of the arctic river. Glaring down at the green liquid, I took a deep breath and waded in. A small groan leaked from my lips as the cold seeped its way into my bones.

I missed Texas.

Amerie glanced back and smirked. Rolling my eyes, I submerged myself under the murky water and went to my happy place as Amerie, the fish on steroids, darted forward.

I stepped onto the frost-covered riverbank and tried to even out my breathing.

Adjusting her gear, Amerie gave me a wicked grin. "What's the matter, Kid?"

Scowling, I resisted the urge to flip her off.

Jasper pulled the map out and briefly looked over it before meeting my gaze.

A smile slowly curved my lips as I turned to Amerie. "Who's ready for a hike?"

"Bloody hell."

I glanced sideways at Parker. "What's the matter, Hollywood, break a nail?" I snickered as I passed him to take my turn in the lead. I stepped over some loose shale and scanned the area with my night vision.

"Bloody hell," he grumbled again as he slipped on the ever-shifting rocks.

Chuckling, I glanced at the sun peeking over the tree lines and then back at the unstable ground. Even with the growing glow I still needed my night vision to safely maneuver across the shifty terrain.

Placing one foot in front of the other, I slowly made my way up the mountain. I could ignore the ragged puffs that hovered in front of my lips and how my shirt clung to my sweaty and river water-soaked skin, but the burn in my exhausted muscles proved more difficult to tune out. My thighs and calves felt as if I had spent several days at Coronado running through the thick sand while carrying someone on my back.

Gritting my teeth against the freezing wind, I pushed the discomfort from my brain and placed a foot down.

One step at a time...

Behind me, Amerie let out a breathy sigh and then started humming a low tune. My lips curved up when her soft hum transformed into a mumbled song, mixing *Rocket Man* and *Straight On* together. "Rocket Man, we are coming for you," Amerie grumbled in a raspy voice. A huff disrupted her remix as the slope became drastically steeper.

Unable to hold it back any longer, laughter erupted from my lips, abruptly ending Amerie's song. "An Elton John, Heart mash-up?" I arched an eyebrow. "Now I've heard it all."

Sterling chuckled. "I kind of liked it."

Amerie gave me a pointed look. "Thank you, *Joker*."

Laughing, I glanced down at the loose rocks as I eased down the steep slope. "I didn't say I didn't like it." My boots slipped on the shale, causing my body to slide a few feet down the mountain. "It's actually quite catchy."

And accurate.

A wicked grin curved my lips.

Rocket Man, here we come.

THE SUN'S rays beamed directly overhead as we entered a small valley. The wind whistled through the trees, bringing a strong odor with it. The rancid smell nearly caused my eyes to water. Covering my nose with my hand, I looked around. In front of me, Jasper moved into the shadows to scan the area.

Suspicion and adrenaline flowed through my veins.

Shifting my stance, I concealed my body behind a thick bush and pulled my M4 out in front of me. From the corner of my eye, I glimpsed Sterling taking out the mini-drone and clicking a few buttons.

A frown marred his usually carefree face. "Bloody drone won't even turn on."

"Yeah," Emersyn whispered. "Comms and sat phone went out a day ago."

Looks like we found our target.

Before anyone could say anything, the distinct sound of shouting male voices drifted over us. Crouching low, I looked through my scope, searching for the threat.

"People shouldn't be this far out," Dee whispered.

No one answered.

No one needed to.

The voices began to fade away, and I straightened up. In front of me, Jasper eased out of the shadows.

His head tilted toward the ridge we just climbed down.

"Bookie, Joker, see if the drone will work up there." His gaze moved to me. "Kid, you and Legacy go track down whoever that was. The rest of us will find a campsite."

I nodded. "Meet here in an hour?"

Jasper looked to Emersyn and Sterling before nodding. "We may not be able to communicate with one another, but the way sound travels here, we should hear if anyone runs into trouble."

Amerie started walking deeper into the forest. "Sounds like a fool-proof plan to me."

I caught the slight lift of Jasper's lips as I jogged past him to catch up to Amerie. "Remember, report back in an hour," he called out. "If you're late, I will come looking for you two."

Amerie kept moving forward. "Yeah, yeah, J...we got it." She glanced down at me with a wicked glint in her green eyes. "Let's go hunting."

We weaved through the shadows, prowling after the fading voices. The farther we traveled into the forest, the harder it became to breathe. I resisted the urge to gag as human waste and body odor filled my nose. Peering through my water-filled eyes, I watched Amerie slow to a crawl.

"Target in sight," she growled softly.

I eased behind a tree next to her and peered around it.

Bile filled my mouth.

A hundred yards across from us, four men dressed in fatigues marched six half-starved men in threadbare clothes. The weakest looking of the group stumbled and fell to his knees. One of the guards rushed forward and waved his gun at the man's face as he yelled a torrent of furious Korean.

I clenched my fists as the man slowly rose to his feet. My gaze wandered over his bare feet and skinny frame. After my time in Damascus, I thought I had seen it all, but this...

The group continued moving forward down a well-trodden path. Keeping to the shadows, Amerie and I silently followed. Before long, they led us to a clearing in the dense woods.

Amerie gasped. "Holy shit."

I could only nod as I stared, wide-eyed, at the massive warehouse in front of us. The guards pushed the group through a set of double doors and then disappeared from view.

"That thing is like the size of two football fields. What do you think is in there?"

Still glaring at the warehouse, she shook her head. "Something that requires workers."

Clenching my fists, I looked around. "There's a path leading to the south."

Amerie nodded. "We still have twenty minutes before meeting with the others. Let's—"

Before she could finish her sentence, another group of six men hobbled out of the warehouse followed by two armed guards. We watched the group slowly trudge across the frost-covered ground.

"Let's follow them," Amerie said so low I barely heard her.

Silently, we stalked the small entourage. My gaze moved from the guards to the red footprints trailing the group. Anger surged through me. I felt my finger twitch toward my trigger, but I resisted the urge to shoot the guards.

Now's not the time, Greer...

A bitter breeze whipped through the trees, bringing a stronger dose of the human waste and filth. I put my hand over my nose and mouth, but it did little to block out the stench. Several times, the rancid odor forced us to stop as we gagged silently into our palms.

A small clearing broke in the trees. Amerie and I stopped at the edge and watched as the group entered an enclosed camp. A barbed wire fence surrounded a community of small stick huts. A couple guards stood stationed in towers while a few others patrolled the perimeters.

My lips pinched together as I took in the number of malnourished men huddled together.

"It's like the prison camps during World War II," I growled.

A few of the prisoners wandered to the fence and walked down its length. I narrowed my eyes at the two men in the front as they hobbled along.

Next to me, Amerie sucked in a breath and lurched forward.

Reaching out, I grasped the edge of her vest and yanked her roughly back into the shadows.

"What the hell, Legacy?" I hissed.

Anger and fear filled her eyes.

Trying to ignore the uneasy feeling in my stomach, I briefly held her gaze and then glanced back at the men walking near the fence.

Oh my God...

My mouth popped open for a moment and then snapped shut as anger consumed me.

Amerie clenched her fists. "They have my brothers."

Chapter 18

"THOSE ASSHOLES HAVE CLARK AND CLINT," AMERIE growled.

I watched as she continued to pace a little path in our camp. She abruptly stopped and folded her arms tightly across her chest. "They are starving to death in there."

Hearing the break in her voice, I chewed on my bottom lip. Amerie's gaze darted around the group before stopping on me. Guilt filled me as she burned me with her desperate gaze.

I took a deep breath. "Amerie…"

She closed her eyes and sighed.

A sharp pang hit my chest, but I ignored it and said the last thing she wanted to hear. "If we try to break them and the rest of the prisoners out now, we compromise the whole mission."

Amerie glared at the ground. "And if it was your brother there?" she whispered in a harsh tone.

My eyes narrowed. "I'd be pissed and hurting just like you are, but I wouldn't compromise the entire mission just for him." She frowned, and I continued in a gentler voice. "We will get them and everyone else out of that hell hole, but first we have to be smart. We need to do some recon. We need to figure out what's in that warehouse, and we're going to need some reinforcements."

Emersyn walked over and bumped Amerie with her

shoulder. "Your brothers will be fine. They grew up with your annoying butt, remember?"

Amerie's lips twitched. She glanced up and met my gaze. The worry and fear remained, but I could also see a determined glint easing its way into her eyes.

She gave me a curt nod. "Where do we start?"

Jasper stepped forward and placed his map down on a boulder. He pointed to a big circle he had drawn. "The warehouse is here." He trailed his finger to the left toward another circle. "And here is the prison camp." He tapped the paper a few times before glancing up. "Break up in teams. Joker, Legacy, Doc, and I will watch the warehouse. Kid, Sheba, Bookie, and Hollywood take the prison camp." Jasper folded the map and placed it in one of his pockets. "I want to know everything. Don't leave out a single detail."

Nodding, I grabbed my gear. As I started to make my way back into the forest, Amerie grabbed my arm. I looked down at her tight grip and arched an eyebrow.

She glanced down at her white knuckles and let her hand fall limply to her side. "What I said back there about your brother…I didn't mean it." She kicked at a small rock on the ground and sighed. "I was pissed and mad, and I shouldn't have said that."

Rolling my eyes, I lightly bumped her shoulder. "It takes more than that to hurt my feelings." At her smirk, I felt my lips lift into a genuine grin as I chuckled softly.

"I get it. If I had been in your shoes, I probably would have done the same thing."

Amerie bobbed her head and took a step back to join her group.

"Hey…" I waited until she turned to meet my gaze. "We're going to get them out of there."

She nodded. "Yeah, I know." Sighing, she glanced back at

Jasper and the others as they prepped to head out. "I know I got stationed at the warehouse with J the babysitter for a reason, but I'm not going to let my emotions hinder me. I can still do my job."

The feeling of déjà vu drifted over me as I recalled a similar conversation back in Damascus.

Crossing my arms, I shook my head. "You don't need a babysitter. We all know you can do your job. That's why you're being sent with J." My gaze shifted to my group heading toward the trees. "You and J have freaky sniper eyes that can see things the rest of us can't." I gave her a quick pat on the shoulder. "Go do your thing and make those assholes pay."

I watched the fire reignite in her eyes and then quickly jogged after my group.

When I reached Parker's side, he asked, "How's she holding up?"

"She's good."

Parker nodded. "Good."

Leading our group, I crept forward. A slight breeze pushed against my face, bringing a whiff of the foul prison camp. Behind me, I heard Dee gag.

"You'd better plug your nose or something, Sheba, because it's going to get a lot worse."

Nodding, she reached into her med bag and pulled out some gauze, but before she could plug her nose, another breeze rushed in with a stronger dose of the rancid smell. Her face convulsed, and she doubled over. My own eyes began to water as I watched Dee fight to keep the contents of her stomach from coming out. Both Emersyn and Parker were covering their noses and mouths with their hands.

"Bloody hell," Parker mumbled.

I waited until everyone seemed in control of their stomachs before I began creeping forward again. The smell grew more potent as the dense packing of trees began to thin.

"Target in sight," I whispered.

I leaned behind a thick tree trunk and scanned the area. The same number of guards still paced along parts of the barbed wire fence while one stood watch in each of the towers. On the ground, the frail men huddled together. They formed a thick mass of bodies, flooding out of the stick huts.

My stomach twisted, and I had to focus on not vomiting.

Emersyn crouched down next to me, her lips pinched and eyes narrowed. "We have to get them out."

"We will."

She didn't respond. Her clenched hands shook slightly as she glared at the prison.

"You good, Bookie?"

She gave a slight shake of her head before nodding. "Just makes me think of my great-great-grandparents, you know."

I frowned. "They were in the concentration camps."

She nodded.

Movement flashed out of my peripheral vision. I turned and saw a group of men moving around the fence line just like Amerie's brothers had earlier.

I drummed my fingers against the side of my M4 and then crouched forward. "I'm going to get a better look at this place."

Parker moved to my side. "I'm coming with you."

The two of us slowly weaved through the trees, blending in with the shadows. We followed the men around the fence. At the backend of the camp, the group stopped. Two men glanced around while one bent over and braced his hands against his knees.

"What are y'all doing?" I whispered as I pulled my M4 around to look through the scope.

My crosshairs moved to the man bent over. His lips moved subtly as his finger tapped against his knee.

A smirk curved my lips.

A guard strolled into view and immediately started yelling when he noticed the three men. I watched as the bent man stopped tapping his finger and slowly rose to a slightly hunched standing position. The other two wrapped a supportive arm around the "weaker" man, and together they hobbled to the closest stick hut.

Parker rocked back on his heels as a proud glint entered his eyes. "They're timing the guard's switch."

"They're planning an escape." Admiration filled me at the men's resilience.

My gaze swept over the back fence as Parker pulled out a small notepad and pencil. The sound of quick scratches mixed in with our hushed breathing.

Glancing down, I arched an eyebrow at his rough yet accurate sketch. "Wow…" I looked up into his brown eyes. "Didn't know you could draw like that."

Grinning, he flipped the page over. "Years of Mum taking me to art class." He nodded toward my watch. "Time how long it takes the guards to switch, and I'll record."

Nodding, I set the timer and watched the guards move. They completed three rotations before I glanced down at Parker's time sheet.

I frowned at the slow and inconsistent times. "The camp's not that big." My gaze wandered to the front of the camp. "They're wasting a lot of time transitioning." I glanced at Parker. "And walking like an old man Sunday driving."

Parker chuckled. "Time how long it takes them between each house."

Nodding, I looked through my scope and focused on a group of men huddled around the farthest hut. A tall man sitting on the outside tracked the movements of the approaching guard. When the guard walked by the house, the tall man took a stick and hit the side of the hut with it.

Moving my gun, I placed my scope on the next house and watched as another man waited until the guard passed his house before he took a stick and hit the side of his hut. I moved from house to house and watched as each hut kept track of the guard's movements.

Shaking my head, I chuckled. These men didn't need rescuing.

"What?" Parker asked.

"These guys are keeping track of the switches between each house." Chuckling again, I pointed toward his scope. "See for yourself."

Parker grinned. "They're pissed and ready to go home." He peered through his scope and then sucked in a breath.

Darting my gaze back to the camp, my finger hovered over my trigger as I searched for the threat.

I saw nothing.

Next to me, Parker remained tensed.

"What's going on, Hollywood?"

Parker took a deep breath and slowly backed away from his scope. "They have John."

My forehead wrinkled. "Who?"

Parker sighed. "Doc's little brother."

I rocked back on my heels and met his gaze. "Oh…" I forced my mouth to close as I focused my attention back on the prison. Taking a deep breath, I made sure my voice rang with conviction. "We'll get him out."

Parker nodded and then checked the time on his watch. "The others will be getting back soon. We should head out."

I did one last scan of the camp and then followed swiftly behind him. Emersyn and Dee looked up when we reached their hiding spot. Parker wordlessly slinked past them as he made his way back to the campsite.

Emersyn watched his retreating back and then arched an eyebrow at me. "What's wrong with him?"

I sighed. "He saw Doc's little brother."

I didn't wait to see their reactions. Easing past them, I followed Parker. We entered our camp before the other group. Taking off my gear, I rolled my head and shoulders and sat down on a smooth boulder.

Dee took a seat next to me and sighed. "Damascus was pretty screwed up, but this…"

I massaged the back of my neck. "Yeah." Rustling drifted to my ear and I glanced over to see Jasper walking into the camp.

Dee tilted her head toward the group walking in. "Judging by the smile on Legacy's face, something happened."

I could only shake my head when I saw Amerie's bright eyes. "There's no telling."

Amerie walked over and plopped down next to me. This was going to be interesting.

I cocked an eyebrow at her smug expression. "I didn't hear any gunfire or cussing, so what happened to make you so pleased with yourself?"

She leaned back on her hands and smirked. "I talked to Clint."

Dee leaned over me to get a better look at Amerie. "How'd you do that? There are guards everywhere."

I didn't have to look to know Amerie was rolling her eyes. "My brothers and I used to have a secret way to communicate when we were kids."

My lips curved up. I could only imagine all of the trouble those three got into.

Their poor mama…

"You were able to talk without raising any suspicion?" Emersyn asked.

Amerie scoffed. "Do you know who you're talking to right now?"

Rolling my eyes, I failed to restrain my snort. "Are you going to brag all night or tell us what happened?"

"You're no fun." Pouting, she gave a dramatic sigh before giving us the details. "So, every fifteen minutes, a group of men leave the warehouse and go to a small creek about a klick away." Amerie sat up and frowned. "One of the groups had Clint in it."

When she didn't say anything, I nudged her shoulder. "And…"

Shaking her head, she continued. "Figured it'd be our only chance to know what all was going on, so I resorted back to our childhood shenanigans." She smirked. "I thought J was going to have a heart attack."

"I nearly did."

I looked up and saw Jasper walking toward us. Behind him, Parker gently patted Evan on the shoulder.

I bit my lip when Evan's worried eyes met mine. He broke eye contact and looked at the ground. Nodding, he took a deep breath and then followed behind the others.

"So, what exactly is this secret code you and your brothers made up?" Dee asked.

"It's mostly a series of taps that mean certain things." She held up a notepad. "We use Morse code for the more in-depth conversations."

I felt my forehead wrinkle. "How did the guards not hear you?"

"And how did Clint and the others know it was you?" Emersyn added.

"The guards were lazy and not paying attention at all, but

Clint was careful responding. His body blocked his finger from the guards. I could barely hear his taps over the creek's water." She turned to Emersyn and made a face. "I thought you were the smart one of our group."

"Legacy…" I warned.

"Kidding," Amerie amended. "Clint and I have a secret tap sequence that not even Clark knows." The corner of her lip lifted into a sad smile. "He was pretty shocked when he first heard me. It's probably a good thing the guards weren't paying close attention, but he recovered quickly, and then used Morse to tell me about their situation."

"What exactly did your brother tell you?" Jasper asked.

Amerie quickly scanned over what she had written in the notebook. "The warehouse is a holding facility where they are forcing the prisoners to make all of their bombs and ammo. Basically, all of North Korea's weapons are housed under this one facility." She rolled her eyes. "Not very smart if you ask me."

Emersyn folded her arms. "It's exactly what the Americans did during World War II at Pearl Harbor."

Amerie glanced at Emersyn. "Seriously, that's what pops into your head? You're like a walking textbook." She shook her head. "Clint said he and several of the other guys were planning to escape and find a way to get word out. They've been working on ways to get out of that hell hole."

She looked at Jasper and then met all of our gazes. "I think I have an idea. It's a little risky, but if it works, we'll definitely be stabbing the heart of North Korea."

I glanced at the others and saw a determined glint in all of their gazes.

Nodding, I faced Amerie. "Let's hear the plan."

Relief flashed in her eyes. She took a small breath and then quickly jumped into her sales pitch. With each word that passed her lips, I had to fight to keep my mouth from hanging open. Stunned, I watched as she stood halfway through her plan and began dramatically talking with her hands.

This girl…

Amerie placed her hands on her hips when she finished and looked expectantly at us.

No one spoke.

No one moved.

I could only gape at Amerie.

Growing impatient with our silence, Amerie cocked out a hip and crossed her arms. "Well…?"

Dee found her voice first. "A little risky?" She gave a slightly hysterical laugh. "Girl, you and I have vastly different meanings of 'a little.'"

A snicker burst from my lips, earning a glare from Amerie. I covered my mouth with my hand.

Amerie rolled her eyes. "Okay, so it's more than a little risky."

Regaining some of my composure, I nodded. "Yeah, but I think it'll work."

Jasper stepped forward. "I think so too." He glanced down at his watch and then back at our group. "We'll spend tomorrow doing recon." His gaze moved to Amerie's. "And then we'll do it Legacy's way."

Chapter 19

Breathing in the crisp morning air, I watched the sun's beams dance among the hanging icicles. Merged together, they created tiny little stars that reflected across the creek's flowing water.

Amerie sighed. "How can a place so beautiful be so ugly?"

My gaze shifted from the light show to bloodstained pebbles. Broken ice shards lay scattered around the red footprints.

"If Bookie were here, I'm sure she'd come up with some smart, philosophical answer." I shrugged. "I like to think it's just God's way of keeping the balance."

Amerie glared at the blood stains. "Well, I wish he could have kept the balance without involving my brothers."

I glanced at her but didn't say anything. A cool breeze pushed against my face, bringing a refreshing smell of the creek's water. So much better than the prison camp.

My lips twitched as I recalled the amount of gauze Dee had placed in her nostrils this morning. Self-preservation had been the only thing that stopped me from teasing her. I could still feel the heat from her withering glare when she caught me staring.

Amerie's low whistle pulled me from my memories. She bumped my shoulder and nodded at the cliff above the creek.

Boulders and leaning trees jutted out at odd angles on the nearly vertical rock wall.

"Suck to go down that." She wriggled her eyebrows at me. "Wonder what it looks like from the top?"

I rolled my eyes. "Probably a whole lot prettier than Eobu's hidden bunker." Smirking at her glower, I nodded at the notepad lying next to her. "Who came up with this code?"

Amerie's mischievous grin returned. "Clark. We grew up in a small house, so the three of us shared a room. When it was time for bed, we never wanted to go to sleep. We always ended up getting in trouble for staying up."

"So he came up with y'all's code?"

She laughed. "Yeah, and from there we progressed to stealing cookies when Mom wasn't looking or pulling pranks on the neighbors."

"Little hellions." My soft chuckles died down as the seriousness of our situation returned. I glanced over my shoulder where the warehouse loomed. "You think Bookie and Joker can figure out that box interference thing?"

Amerie frowned. "I hope so. Otherwise, the plan may turn more into a suicide mission."

Before I could reply, a foul stench drifted toward us. Wrinkling my nose, I watched a group of five men hobble to the creek while two guards hovered off to the side.

Amerie made two, clipped taps.

The men bent over the creek and started filling their large buckets. I looked over each of them before stopping on a sandy-haired man in the middle. He stood close to the others and tilted away from the guards talking amongst themselves. As he filled up his two buckets, his index finger tapped away. Amerie quickly jotted down the message.

He finished filling his buckets and slowly moved with the others back to the warehouse. As he passed our hiding spot, he softly drummed his fingers against the side of one of his buckets.

Amerie's lips curved up into a wicked grin. Her gaze darted to the guard's retreating backs before she quietly drummed back a similar, shorter version.

I waited until the rancid smell had vanished before I turned to Amerie. "What did he say at the end?"

Amerie grabbed the notepad and stood. "Give them hell." She glanced down at her watch before meeting my gaze. "Come on. J's going to want to hear this."

Back at the camp, Amerie and I were the last ones to join the group. Jasper looked at his watch with a frown but didn't say anything.

Amerie rolled her eyes. "Oh, come on, J..." she huffed. "We're not that late."

"Just ten minutes," I mumbled low, so only Amerie could hear.

She shrugged. "We had a lot of information to get."

Shaking my head, I plopped down on a boulder next to Sterling. He looked at me with a mischievous glint in his eyes.

My lips twitched.

Oh boy, here we go.

Sterling turned toward Jasper. "I think since Bookie and I got here *on time*..." he gave Amerie a pointed look, "...we should tell our information first."

Amerie folded her arms. "What are you? Three?"

Sterling nodded. "And a half."

Jasper opened his mouth, but nothing came out. Shaking his head, he turned to Emersyn. "Well?"

Sterling smirked at Amerie.

"Best for last," she muttered.

I elbowed them both hard. "Pay attention," I hissed.

Completely unfazed by Amerie and Sterling's childish behavior, Emersyn kept her gaze on Jasper. "We located the modem causing the interference, and we can disable it…but I suggest we disable it at the last second."

Evan looked at the sketch Parker had drawn of the device and then looked back at Emersyn. "How come?"

"Right now, it's not only blocking us from communicating with one another, but also the guards." A mischievous grin curved Emersyn's lips. "Why make it any easier for them?"

Amerie bobbed her head. "I like it." She glanced at Jasper with an impatient look.

Shaking his head, he waved a hand at her. "What do you have, Legacy?"

She grinned. "Well, one of the prisoners actually understands Korean. He overheard some of the guards talking about this big showing to the officials." She frowned. "Something big is about to happen. They've tried to stall production as much as they could, but they can only do so much before the guards intervene."

My hands fisted as images of the prisoners' bruised and swollen faces popped into my mind.

Next to me, Sterling popped his knuckles. "Looks like today's the day."

Parker smirked at his cousin. "We can always count on you to state the obvious."

Chuckling, I shook my head. Some things never changed.

Emersyn chewed loudly on her gum as she stared intently at the map Jasper had pulled out.

Dee caught my eye and smirked. "She's got her thinking cap on," she mouthed.

Suppressing my urge to snicker, I stood and walked over to Jasper. "What do you think?"

Looking at the map, he tapped his finger against the boulder before answering, "Bookie, you said it'd take about a day-and-a-half trek to get the comms up to talk with Washington?"

Emersyn nodded. "Give or take a few hours."

Jasper released a long exhale. "It's the only plan we have," he mumbled so low I barely heard him. Looking up at our little dysfunctional family, he gave a curt nod. "Let's do this. Joker, Bookie, Doc, you three head out and get Washington on board. The rest of us will get everything ready."

Parker and Dee helped Evan and Emersyn pack their gear while Amerie and Sterling headed toward the snack bag, laughing and talking with their hands. I shook my head at the two goofballs and then shifted my attention to Jasper, who stared silently at the map.

I lightly punched his shoulder. "You good?"

His eyes never strayed from the map. "Yeah."

I waited for him to say more, but when he didn't, I gently tugged the map away from him. "I hear a 'but' in that statement." I cocked an eyebrow when he met my gaze. "What's going on?"

He sighed. "Legacy may like winging things, but I like a plan without so many variables and what ifs…"

I laughed dryly. "Trust me, so do I, but like you said, J, it's the only plan we have."

"You know if just one little thing goes wrong…"

I placed my hand on his shoulder, cutting him off. "We'll fight like hell." I nodded at our group. "No matter what happens."

Chapter 20

I STARED AT THE PIECE OF PAPER, GRIPPING MY PENCIL tightly. The longer I stared the more frustrated I became.

It shouldn't have been hard to write a letter home, but no matter how hard I tried, the words just wouldn't come.

"Writer's block?"

I spun around and noticed Dee leaning against a tree. Scowling, I shoved the blank paper and pencil into my gear bag.

"How long have you been standing there?"

Dee pushed away from the tree and walked toward me. "Long enough."

My lips pursed as I glowered at my bag. I should have been more aware. Rookie mistake.

Dee plopped down next to me on the boulder and glanced at my bag, where part of the blank paper peeked out.

"You should write that letter."

My lips formed a thin line. Crossing my arms, I leaned against the side of the mountain.

"What's the point?" I gave Dee a side glance and shrugged. "I don't plan on dying."

She didn't smile at my horrible joke.

Sighing, I once again turned my glower back on the page. "I don't know what to say to them," I whispered. "I love you? Sorry I couldn't keep my promise?" I looked back at Dee. "I mean, what did you say to your family?"

She leaned her back against the mountainside and sighed. "The truth…what they'd want to hear. We don't ever plan on dying, but something about this mission just feels different." She crossed her arms and stared at the thick bundle of trees, shielding us from wandering eyes. "We've been in a lot of dangerous situations before, and we've had some pretty crazy plans, but this…"

I thought about Amerie's "a little" risky plan. Of their own accord, my eyes drifted back to the paper.

Dee noticed my gaze and frowned. "I don't plan on me or any of us dying, but just in case something does happen, I find peace knowing my family will have at least some closure from my letter."

I nodded.

Out of the corner of my eye, I saw Dee's lips start to tip up. "*And*…I don't plan on my family ever reading that letter. I know Legacy thinks it's bad luck to write a letter like that, but I don't see it as being any different than those last phone calls we always make before deploying."

My lips began to curve up as what she said hit me. Technically, I had written this letter before.

Dee's own smile grew. "Besides, we're all so stubborn, having that letter in our pockets will probably be the thing that pisses us off enough to find the will to keep breathing."

I chuckled. "Never out of the fight."

"Never out of the fight."

"I noticed you wrote two letters. Who was the second one for?"

She didn't answer at first. A light blush tinted her cheeks as she said softly, "My boyfriend, Jason."

My mouth dropped.

I had known Dee now for nine months, I thought of her as

my sister, but I had no idea she was dating anyone. I had assumed, like the rest of us, she was single.

She shrugged. "It's not something I ever liked talking about." She chuckled at my wrinkled forehead. "We started dating our freshman year of high school. Even talked about getting married before the draft and still enlisting, but I shot down that idea. My granny would have died if we had a quick wedding at the courthouse. If you ever meet my granny, you'll understand. She doesn't do anything halfway, especially parties."

She suddenly looked sad. "I can handle us going to hell-holes like this. That's fine. Give it to me all day long, but knowing Jason is out there in a place that wants to kill him...I just can't do it. I have a hard time breathing every time it crosses my mind."

I nodded, thinking of Charles. "I get it."

"He's in the Air Force. I never know where he's at, and he never knows where I'm at, and that's how we want it."

I studied her face. "That must make it hard on y'all. How do y'all talk?"

"We rely on emails mainly." A smile began to form on her lips. "He also sends me a lot of letters. He's kind of old school, says a letter is more personal, something I can feel and hold onto." She wriggled her eyebrows at me. "Sometimes he even sprays some of his cologne on it."

I snorted. "How romantic."

She chuckled. "His grandfather did that for his grandmother, and I always thought it was the most romantic thing. She still has a box filled with the letters he sent her."

"That is special," I said with a smile.

We sat there in silence for several minutes. The cold wind slashed at us, but the sun's warm rays soothed the lashings. I tilted my head toward the sunshine and closed my eyes. Breathing deeply, I rolled my head and shoulders.

"You know, if we weren't surrounded by our enemies, this place wouldn't be so bad." I glanced around the countryside and smiled. "It really is quite beautiful here."

Dee grimaced at the melting snow that covered the trees and rocks. "I don't understand you nature freaks."

I laughed. "I forgot. Unless its glamping, you hate it."

Dee rolled her eyes. "Just because I appreciate taking a shower every day and having an actual mattress to lie down on every night does not make me some pampered, prissy princess."

I held my hands up. "Hey, I didn't say anything."

"But you were thinking it."

"It may not make you a pampered, prissy princess, but it does make you a sassy, spirited Sheba."

Dee shrugged. "I don't hear any insults there."

Laughing, I leaned back and let the moment wash away all of my worries and fears, and just for a second, I let myself believe I was out on a camping trip with one of my best friends.

There was no war.

No prison camp starving people I cared about.

It was just my friends, nature, and me.

But all too soon, I knew I'd have to face reality.

My smile fading, I turned back to Dee. "Did you and Hollywood find a good spot?"

Dee nodded. "Yeah, it'll be just far enough away from the blast and will provide good cover if something goes wrong."

"Hard to believe this time tomorrow it'll all be over."

"Yeah, one way or another..." Dee patted my knee before standing up. She tilted her head toward my bag. "Write that letter."

I watched her disappear into the trees before glancing at my bag. Sighing, I reached down and grabbed the blank page. It felt heavy, making me want to drop it, but I forced myself to hold on.

Just another phone call home...

Pencil in hand, I breathed deeply and then let the words flow freely, making them as carefree and light as possible. I knew, despite my wishes, eyes would not be dry as they read my goodbye.

Chuckling, I quickly added a joke about having the Kleenex close by. I had no intention of this letter ever being read by my family, but just in case things didn't pan out, I wanted to provide some comical relief.

Signing my name, I reread the page several times, checking to make sure I didn't leave anything unsaid. As I reached the end of my letter, a serene calm washed over me and I let out a relieved breath.

I needed that.

I folded the letter up nicely and placed it in the pocket close to my heart.

As I scanned the tree line, adrenaline started pumping through my veins.

Shouldering my bag, I stood up and started making my way back to camp.

Time for work.

Chapter 21

I RAN MY FINGERS OVER THE SMOOTH BULLET AS THE SUN warmed the back of my skin. Squatting down, I continued to load my clips with rounds.

Dee plopped down next to me. I spared her a quick glance, but stayed focused on my task.

She watched me work for several minutes before sighing. "I can't wait to get off this God-forsaken mountain."

I smirked at the longing in her voice. "What's the matter? It's not like there were any snakes on it."

Dee folded her arms and glared at me. "There also haven't been any beds, warm water, toilets, decent food…" Raising her arm, Dee sniffed and then grimaced. "It's going to take months before I start smelling like a human again."

I snickered as I took in her dirt-covered body. "Probably more like a year."

Dee glowered.

I looked back at my gear and smiled. "In a few hours, the others will be back, and we should be receiving the go-ahead to finish these assholes. Then you can take as many hot showers as your big ol' Sheba heart desires."

A blissful expression popped up on Dee's face. "Can't wait." Her carefree look only lasted a second before she became serious again. Picking up a bullet, she held it a moment before handing it to me. "You think we'll be given the go-ahead?"

Halting my movements, I took my time to answer her.

I didn't need to be as smart as Emersyn to know Washington wouldn't be thrilled when they heard Amerie's plan. Hell, when I first heard it, a part of me wanted to put Amerie in a straitjacket, but the other part of me knew it was our only option.

I sighed. "Honestly, I have no idea." I finished loading my last bullet and shrugged. "They wanted us to strike the heart of North Korea...they'll be getting exactly what they asked for."

Dee opened her mouth but quickly shut it as she jumped to her feet. Spinning around, I whipped my SIG out and faced the incoming threat.

A panting Amerie and Parker sprinted into the camp. I scanned the woods behind them, searching for any pursuers.

"What's wrong?" Jasper demanded as he quickly made his way to Amerie.

"How far out are the others?" Amerie asked breathlessly. A vein in her temple pounded as she tried to slow her breathing.

Jasper frowned. "If they didn't run into any problems, still about two hours, most likely three."

"Shit." Parker's muscles tensed as he clenched his fists.

"Clark said the North Koreans are planning to launch an attack on DC today. A few of the bigwigs are coming down to oversee it," she rushed out.

"Do they know when?"

Already I was trying to do the math in my head, trying to figure out if our own attack would beat theirs or not.

"In the next hour or two...whenever those head assholes roll in."

My stomach clenched.

I turned to Jasper. "There's no way we'll get to them

before then. Even assuming Washington approves our plan and gives the go-ahead, that won't happen until tonight."

Jasper nodded. "I know." His gaze swept over our small group, but he didn't say anything else.

He didn't need to.

We already knew.

We were missing nearly half our team, we were outmanned and outgunned. We had no backup, no way to communicate with one another, and there was no way for us to warn our officials back home.

I took a deep breath and looked at my teammates.

We'd fight like hell until the end.

Jasper met my gaze. "Plan stays the same. We just need to make a few minor adjustments."

My lips curved up into a wicked grin. "Let's go even the odds a bit."

Chapter 22

SPRINTING THROUGH THE SNOW-COVERED FOREST, I COULD feel time slipping away as I tried to beat the next wave of prisoners at the creek. They were the crucial first step to this crazy plan working. Without them, we would die.

Not going to happen...

Bowing my head, I picked up speed and pushed my body even harder. The soft trickle of a running stream filled the silent woods, and I gradually began to slow my pace.

Blending in with the shadows of a towering tree, I scanned the area for any approaching guards. Seeing none, I stepped out of the tree's protection and pulled out mine and the others' extra SIGs.

A few feet from the stream, I found the overgrown bush Amerie had told me about. Straining to hear any approaching movements, I quickly placed the five guns under the bush's protection.

Once satisfied a guard wouldn't accidentally spy the weapons, I melted back into the shadows and waited. A moment later, the sound of trudging feet and the scent of body odor and chemicals drifted toward me.

My stomach churned as the prisoners limped into view, a few of the weaker ones stumbling. Clenching my teeth, I slid my gaze to the two guards.

The taller one strolled toward a tree across from me and leaned against it as he pulled out a cigarette. His friend walked over and shook his head. He said something to the smoking guard, making him shrug.

While they had their little conversation, I tapped out a quick message alerting the men to the situation and the job we needed them to do. The sturdiest man in the group gave a slight nod.

Leaving his buckets next to the stream, he walked over to the bush where I had stashed the guns. The guard arguing with the smoker immediately turned on the man. Shifting slightly, I lined the guard in my sights as he stormed toward the man.

He held up his hands. "Easy, I just have to take a shit." He motioned toward the bush and then his pants.

The guard glanced back and forth between the man and the bush with a glower. A few seconds passed before the smoker pushed off the tree.

I couldn't understand the words he was saying, but judging from his tone, he was helping us out. The stricter guard narrowed his eyes but eventually waved a hand at the man.

The smoker shoved a cigarette at the other guard and then laughed when he pushed it away. The prisoner walked behind the bush and slowly started to squat down. Keeping the guards in his sight, he slowly inched his hand toward the hidden guns.

The guards had their backs to the man as they continued to argue. The man quickly grabbed two of the guns and had them hidden before I could even blink. He took a few extra seconds to make sure the remaining three guns were hidden from view before slowly rising up and making his way back to the others filling their buckets. He glanced at the other prisoners and winked.

Give them hell, I tapped out.

The smoking guard flicked his cigarette away and then ordered the prisoners to march out. The five men did as they were told, but I couldn't miss the way they held themselves higher and with more confidence. The glint in all of their eyes screamed determination and retribution. As they passed me, the man turned his head slightly toward me and gave a slight nod.

A sardonic smile lifted my lips.

I waited until I could no longer hear their footsteps before sprinting toward the prisoner camp where the others waited. As I ran, my gaze darted down to my watch.

Grunting, I picked up my speed. As if God knew my desperation, a strong breeze pushed from behind, propelling me forward.

Snow crunched under my feet as my breathing became more labored. Slinking through the trees, the distinct smell of waste and filth made its way to my nose. I brought a hand to my mouth as I ran, trying to block out some of the stench.

Releasing a breath, I slowed my stride to a jog as the dense trees began to thin. My breathing came out in ragged pants, but I took a deep breath and then whistled our signal. It came out weak and garbled, but it did its job.

Out about five yards, Jasper let out the same bird-sounding whistle. I crouched down and slowly eased my way toward him. He was lying flat on his stomach and had the front tower guard lined up in his sights. The man in the tower had his back to the prison while the other guards went about their routines, completely oblivious to the danger just outside their fence.

"Weapons secured," I whispered.

Jasper gave a curt nod, never taking his eyes off the guard. "Good. Get in position."

Nodding, I quickly weaved through the thick foliage and trees, scanning the ground for my sign.

Where'd you put me, Amerie?

Slowing my movements, I noticed a pile of rocks near a tree. My lips stretched into a wide grin when I noticed a large Q and B at the base of the tree.

"Oh, Legacy…" I crouched down and pulled my M4 in front of me and watched as a guard strolled past. "The Queen Bs are here, assholes."

Across from me, a group of prisoners casually leaned against their stick hut. Flipping on my laser, I peered through my sites and found Clark standing in the middle of the group. I placed a red dot in the center of his chest and moved it back and forth. As soon as he saw my signal, I clicked my laser off.

Clark and another prisoner pushed away from the house and started walking toward the front of the camp. Even from where I hid, I could hear Clark and the blond belting out, Elton John's *Rocket Man*.

A small snicker leaked from my lips.

Nice choice.

Obviously, Amerie wasn't the only Anderson with a twisted sense of humor. Now I knew where she got it from.

Several guards walked out of the nicest looking house in the camp. Their shouting mixed in with the taunting rendition of the seventies hit. I moved my gaze from the distraction and lined my target up.

Grunts of pain filtered to my ears. Clenching my teeth, I waited.

"Assholes," I mumbled.

I inhaled deeply and continued to track my target through my scope. He had just passed the stick hut when I saw my sign.

My guard turned his head toward the prisoners standing around the hut. His stride faltered as he looked at them. Before he could turn his head, I pulled the trigger.

His body crumbled to the ground.

I stayed just long enough to watch the prisoners strip away all of the guard's weapons before I darted back toward Jasper.

"The back is secured," I said in a low voice when I reached his side.

Easing down beside him, I lined up my next target. I chewed on the inside of my cheek as I waited for Amerie to make the next move.

"This radio silence is killing me," I grumbled under my breath.

Breathing evenly, I kept my target locked in my sights. Another guard walked out of the house and looked around. Even from this distance, I could see his furrowed brow.

"Come on, Legacy," I mumbled.

As if she heard me, the man fell limply to the ground. I squeezed the trigger and dropped my target before he could even utter a sound. Next to me, Jasper fired at the front tower guard, who callously watched the guards beat Clark and the blonde, clueless to his surroundings.

The man's body fell from the tower and crashed to the ground.

Shouts sounded as guards scrambled out of the main house. Confusion swept over their features as they were fired on from every angle. I lined up a chubby guard I had watched beat several prisoners, but before I could pull the trigger, he crumbled to the ground. I moved my sights to another guard and fired. Next to me, Jasper took out a guard trying to slink back into the house.

As quickly as the firing had started, it ended. A layer of

smoke hovered over the area. I scanned the camp, searching for any remaining guards.

"Clear," Jasper said.

I looked over the area once more and then nodded. "Clear."

Together we stood and made our way into the camp. Dee and Parker met us at the front gate.

"Well, that worked out pretty good," Parker quipped.

I snorted and grinned at him.

Clark reached us as we made it to the front of the guard's house. Blood dribbled down his smiling face as he gave me a fist bump. "Nice work."

Behind him, the stronger of the men were distributing weapons to one another. Clark glanced down at the chubby guard and glared. "Asshole."

My eyes wandered over his beaten face. "You good?"

He nodded.

Clint walked up next to him and shook his head. "You look a lot better than you sing."

Before he could make a retort, Amerie rushed over and wrapped her arms around both her brothers. I smiled at the family reunion.

Clark laughed. "Miss us?"

Amerie shoved his shoulder. Her throat bobbed a few times as she looked them over. Clearing her throat, she wrinkled her nose. "Damn, y'all stink."

Dee shook her head. She caught my eye and smiled. "Subtle as always."

I grinned as we made our way into the house. "That's just how she copes."

"I can hear you," Amerie growled.

I laughed at the weak anger in her voice. Nothing could dim her mood right now.

Jasper, Parker, and a few of the other men were already in the house searching for intel and extra weapons. Seeing they had it under control, I grabbed the first aid kit hanging on the wall and walked back outside.

All of the men were severely malnourished and dehydrated. There were about ten who looked like they could barely stand upright, but the glint in their eyes told me they had just enough energy to get out of here.

As I wandered through the men, I noticed several cuts and bruises, but nothing life-threatening. I had just reached the end of the group when I noticed the man who had sung with Clark. Blood ran from his nose and his arm hung at an odd angle.

Walking toward him, I nodded at his shoulder. "Let me take a look at that."

The man gave me a crooked smile. "Well, I'm not going to object to a pretty girl checking me over."

Snorting, I rolled my eyes. "Easy there, Casanova."

When I reached his side, his smile grew. I stopped and narrowed my eyes at him as my forehead wrinkled.

He cocked an eyebrow. "Problem?"

Something about the man reminded me of someone, but I had no idea who.

Shaking my head, I set the kit down. "You just looked familiar."

The man chuckled and shook his head. "I wouldn't have forgotten that pretty face of yours or cute little accent."

I scoffed. "I'm not the one with an accent."

His crooked smile came back out, and it suddenly dawned on me why he looked so familiar; Evan had the same uneven smile.

"You wouldn't happen to have a brother named Doc,

would you?" I shook my head, realizing he may not know the nickname. "Evan, I mean."

The man's face fell as he looked around the area. "He's my older brother." He stopped scanning the area and met my gaze again. "Is he okay? I didn't see him with Jasper."

I nodded. "Yeah, he's fine. He should be showing up to the party soon."

While he was distracted by my words, I popped his dislocated shoulder back into place.

"Bloody hell!" He gritted his teeth and narrowed his eyes at me. "No warning?"

Biting the inside of my cheek to keep from laughing, I shrugged. "It would have just made it worse."

Before he could make a retort, a low rumbling drifted over us. I pulled my M4 around and glanced at the sound.

"Please tell me that's my brother making his entrance…"

I shook my head. "I wish." My muscles started to tense as I checked my watch. "It's way too early for him."

Jasper came out of the house with a gym bag. He glanced at the approaching cloud of dust and the dead guards scattered across the ground.

He looked right at me. "Exfil now."

The words had barely left his mouth before he started assisting the weaker men toward the gate. Stuffing the rest of the gauze and medical wraps in my med bag, I turned toward John. My eyes drifted over his battered face to his hand cradling his newly relocated shoulder.

"You good to go?"

His lips curled up as a wicked glint appeared in his eyes. "Thought you'd never ask."

A wave of admiration drifted through me. "Good." I helped a man with a twisted knee and swollen face stand on wobbly feet. Gently, I guided the man toward John's good arm and kept him balanced until John wrapped a supportive grip around the man's emaciated waist.

"I'm going to need you to help Sheba and Clint get these men to our campsite." I bent down and picked up the pistol from a dead guard. "Hope you shoot better than you sing."

John took the gun from my hands. "These bloody wankers are about to get everything they deserve."

I smiled as we hobbled out of the camp. "Hell yeah, they are."

John winked. "And for the record, my singing is beautiful."

My scoff at his words broke off as I took in the dried blood covering old bruises and the goose egg already appearing on his forehead. Anger filled me as I thought of the torture he had gone through.

He deserved some retribution…they all did.

And they were going to get it.

We made it to the edge of the forest, and I helped maneuver John and the other man toward Dee. Off to the side, Amerie kneeled with her muzzle pointed at the incoming convoy.

"I've got a shot on the lead driver," she stated calmly.

I skimmed over the injured men. Only about half of them were going to be strong enough to help us fight. The other half barely had the strength to support their own weight. There was no way they'd make it if we started a gunfight now.

Jasper came to the same conclusion as me. "Stand down. The injured need more time to make it to base."

Reaching around, I pulled my M4 out in front of me. John looked back and met my gaze. "Take care of yourself, girly." He smiled and winked. "I want to see that pretty face at the end of this."

Rolling my eyes, I waved him off. "Get out of here, Casanova."

The sound of shuffling footsteps and low moans pierced my ears over the snarling vehicles. I crouched down and eased myself up to where Amerie kneeled.

Looking through my scope, I saw five large trucks blazing toward us. I kicked off my safety.

"Ready, Legacy?"

Her finger flexed around the trigger. "Those assholes are going to pay for what they did to my brothers."

Behind us, I could hear Jasper ordering the remaining men strong enough to fight to go with Parker to the warehouse while Clark and a few others disappeared in the trees.

"You think they'll have enough time to make it through the woods if this goes south?"

I chewed on my lip. "Their adrenaline will kick in... they'll do whatever it takes to get the job done." As the words left my mouth, I knew they were true.

I felt rather than saw Amerie's nod.

The cloud of dust descended on us as the lead vehicle stormed over the hill.

"Legacy," Jasper ordered.

Gunpowder filled my nose as her bullet whizzed through the air. I heard the sound of shattered glass followed by screeching tires as the vehicles came to an abrupt stop.

Shouts erupted into the air.

I pulled my trigger, quickly taking out the man in the passenger seat. Like a horde of furious fire ants, men piled out of the back of the truck.

Bullets rained down on us.

I ducked behind a tree just as two vehicles near the middle of the pack raced backwards and then accelerated back down the mountain.

"I'll give you three guesses who was in that truck," Amerie shouted as she took out another Korean.

I gritted my teeth as a flying piece of bark sliced through my forearm. Taking aim, I lined up the asshole who hit my tree and watched as he crumbled to the ground.

"Wish they would have stayed," I growled.

Amerie laughed viciously. "Me too. I would have loved having the chance to take the head off this snake."

Before the chuckle could pass my lips, another large truck came flying in. A wall of dust billowed up as bullets pummeled the area. Twenty more men jumped out and began firing.

Out of the corner of my eye, I noticed several soldiers trying to flank us. I swiveled my muzzle around toward them and lined the first one in my sights. As soon as he fell, I lined the second one up and then the third. When all three bodies lay motionless in the snow, I moved my attention back to the other fire ants and frowned.

"Legacy, fall back," I ordered.

Nodding, she eased up into a crouch and we eased backward.

"How we looking, J?" Amerie yelled.

"Clear right. Clear right."

We moved back to the right and found another tree to shoot from. Sweat trailed down my face as I lined up targets. A man began easing his way toward us. He walked into my crosshairs, and I pulled the trigger.

"Shit!" Amerie yelped in pain.

Keeping my eyes on my approaching targets, my crosshairs found another target.

"Legacy?" I shouted.

Her labored breathing filled my ears.

Worry pooled in my stomach. I darted a glance over my

shoulder and noticed a trail of blood oozing from the side of her thigh.

Amerie gritted her teeth. "I'm good," she hissed as she began firing again.

I lingered on her wound for a second longer before I lined another man in my sights.

"Comms should be back up soon," I yelled over the roar of gunfire.

Instead of answering, Amerie took out two more men.

A lull in the firing drifted over us.

"We need to fall back again," Amerie whispered.

Nodding, I darted back with her. She gave me a side glance.

My stomach knotted at the look in her eyes.

"Something didn't go as planned. Comms should have been back up by now," she whispered.

Before I could answer, burning flames erupted in my shoulder. I stumbled back and leaned against a thick tree trunk for support. Looking down, I saw a quarter-sized hole leaking dark liquid.

"Kid?" Amerie continued to fire back at the swarming ants while she yelled at me. "You okay."

Grimacing, I nodded. "Yeah, I'm good."

Off to the right, I saw Jasper firing away.

They just kept coming.

Ignoring the stabbing pain, I moved my crosshairs onto another target.

Lord, please help us…

We needed our comms back.

We needed backup.

We needed a miracle.

Chapter 23

"FALL BACK!" JASPER SHOUTED.

Still shooting, I eased backward. From the corner of my eye, I noticed Amerie's grimace as she limped back.

"Move it, Legacy!" I shouted as I stepped in front of her. "Get to that tree line!"

She grumbled under her breath something about me overreacting and being fine, but she did as I ordered.

Bullets continued to bounce all around us, kicking up rocks that rammed into my skin. My eyes narrowed as I lined up the culprit.

"Clear, Kid, move it," Jasper ordered.

Pushing off my tree, I sprinted toward Jasper and Amerie. A bullet whizzed by, causing me to flinch and duck my head. Picking up my speed, I dove behind a boulder and sucked in a breath. I reached into my pocket and grabbed another magazine.

"Kid?" Amerie shouted.

"I'm good," I panted.

Crouching low, I began firing again. Adrenaline pumped through my body, blocking out all of the pain and noise. My only focus was centered on the never-ending hoard of bodies swarming toward us.

"We need to get to the warehouse and get comms back up," Amerie stated.

Sweat, dirt, and blood covered her face. Determination sparked in her eyes, but I could also see some worry.

"Your brothers are fine."

Snapping twigs sounded behind us. Raising my M4, I spun around and zoomed in on the approaching threat. How did they get behind us?

My stomach hollowed out.

If the others had failed and the guards from the warehouse were now joining this fight…

"Don't shoot! It's me!" I heard Dee's shout before I saw her.

"Damn it, Sheba!" I glared at her as she kneeled down next to me. "I could have shot you."

She lined someone up and pulled the trigger. "But you didn't."

Shaking my head, I turned back toward the relentless spray of bullets. "That would have been one hell of a phone call to your family," I grumbled.

Dee gave me a side glance and shrugged. Her lips turned down when she saw my blood-covered torso.

"I'm good," I answered before she could ask. A man wandered into my sights and I pulled the trigger. "How are the others?"

Dee grimaced as a flying twig sliced her cheek. "Asshole." She fired a round before answering. "They are safe and secure. I came to help y'all as soon as I had them hidden."

I nodded. At least one part of the plan had worked.

"Another one bites the dust," Amerie sang softly before she began humming the rest of the song.

Shaking my head, I found another target. A breeze brought in a strong new whiff of cordite. Breathing in the familiar smell, I eased backward again.

"J, are we clear right?" I yelled.

Bullets rained down.

Clenching my teeth, I ducked my head low.

Static filled my ears.

"These assholes are really starting to piss me off," Amerie mumbled so low I could barely hear her over the buzzing in my ears.

Static pierced through the noise again.

"Legacy?"

Thank God! They did it!

A fresh swell of confidence and strength renewed my weary muscles when I heard Emersyn's shocked voice in my ear.

"What the heck is going on?" Panting came through the line. "We heard the gunfight and came as fast as we could," Emersyn said, so smoothly I would have thought she was standing still if I didn't know her so well. "We're almost to the camp."

A smile popped onto my face, and I breathed a sigh of relief. "Bookie, you have no idea how good it is to hear your voice."

Snow kicked up next to my feet, spraying my face with the frozen liquid. Swiping the mess away from my eyes, I took aim at the culprit. "Damn fire ants."

Another bullet whizzed over my head, snapping a limb off the tree. The branch crashed down, landing near my feet. Through the comms, I could hear Jasper filling the others in on what had happened.

A shadow flashed past.

Tracking the movement with my muzzle, I found a man getting ready to hurl a grenade at us. I quickly put my crosshairs on him and watched as he dropped lifelessly to the ground.

I heard Jasper order Emersyn to use the sat phone to

request an immediate airstrike. Out of my peripheral vision, I saw Dee's head snap toward Jasper.

"Hey, at least if we go down, we take those assholes with us." The words had just passed my lips when a huge explosion went off.

What the hell?

Ducking low, I peeked around my trunk and saw a string of ripped bodies strewn around the man I had just shot. The grenade offered half a breath of relief from the bullets before another swarm replaced the ones lying on the ground.

"You've got to be kidding me..." I huffed. "They just keep coming."

"We've gotta move!" Amerie yelled.

"J, are we clear on the right?" I shouted again.

"Negative. Move left, I repeat, move left!"

"Ah shit," I groaned.

Frowning, I noticed Dee's expression mirrored my own.

"There's nothing to the left but that damn cliff," she growled.

Tree bark and gravel kicked up around us, providing all the encouragement I needed to get up and move. "Yeah, well, we're dead if we stay here."

Keeping my head low, I zigzagged through the trees as fast as my feet could carry me. Next to me, Dee cursed as her hand whipped up to clutch her side. Blood pooled around her fingers, quickly covering them in a thick red liquid.

She clenched her teeth in pain but never slowed down. Half turned, she fired twice at the unrelenting Koreans.

Reaching toward my vest, I pulled out a grenade and threw it as hard as I could. My shoulder screamed in protest, but I ignored its shouts. A loud boom filled my ears, followed by a cloud of snow and dust flying into the air.

A group of motionless men lay scattered on the ground.

The spraying bullets halted, allowing us a quick moment of peace.

"We could really use some help down here," Parker called out in an exhausted voice.

"We're almost to the warehouse," Sterling answered immediately.

Inhaling deeply, I gave a tired nod. I knew the prisoner soldiers would fight like hell, but I also knew their bodies weren't going to offer them much support.

Our ragged group reached the edge of the cliff, and I looked down. My stomach dropped at the sight. Jumping out of a plane with a parachute didn't seem so bad anymore.

Jasper glanced down the cliff and then over our battered bodies. We were all covered in dirt and blood. Our labored breaths filled the air. Behind me, I could hear the faint sound of snapping twigs and crunching leaves of approaching heavy footsteps. How the hell had they caught up so fast?

"This is the quickest way to the others," Jasper stated.

An almost hysterical laugh escaped my lips. "Aren't we supposed to be going away from the massive explosive site, not toward it?"

A muscle twitched in Jasper's mouth. "Tell them that." His gaze wandered over my head to where the growing sound of approaching footsteps loomed.

Amerie stepped up next to me. "We've got to help them, and this is the only way down." The usual humor in her voice had been replaced with tension. I knew she could only see her brothers down there.

"We're going to help them," I stated.

Amerie nodded. The worry began to seep away as her typical spark began to shine through again. She smirked mischievously at me. "Good thing none of us are scared of heights." She nudged my shoulder, causing a pained hiss to rush from my lips. "'Cause then it'd really suck to go down this thing."

Narrowing my eyes at her, I shoved her toward the edge. "Go on, crippled. Your slow ass needs to go down first. I doubt these assholes are going to wait for you."

Rolling her eyes, she waved her middle finger at me. Amusement revived my weary muscles as Amerie's charm worked its magic.

Dee followed behind Amerie as I turned back toward the trees. The relentless ants hadn't made their way to us yet, but I knew it was just a matter of minutes before they began swarming again.

"We'll let them get partway down and then we'll go," Jasper said as he took a position beside me.

He moved his muzzle toward the tree line. Blood trickled down his leg and pooled on the top of his boot. I glanced at the trees and then bent down and grabbed a handful of snow packed dirt.

Better than nothing.

Brushing out most of the grass and leaves, I packed it in the quarter-sized hole in his thigh.

Cursing, he glared down at me.

I shrugged. "Beats bleeding to death." I grimaced as I did the same to my shoulder.

The sound of approaching footsteps became louder.

I glanced down to see both Amerie and Dee were almost a quarter of the way down.

"We'd better go now, before the bullets start flying."

Jasper nodded. He squatted down and looked over his shoulder at me with an arched eyebrow. "Waiting for an invitation?"

Breathing deeply, I mimicked his actions. My butt slid across the slick rock slab. The air whooshed from my lungs as I dropped a few feet down the side of the mountain. My feet crashed into the rocky side, jarring every bone in my body.

My heart pounded rapidly in my chest as I focused on leaning backward to keep from somersaulting down the cliff. Digging my fingers into the ground, I tried to control my descent over the steep terrain. Gravel and tree branches scraped my legs and arms, tearing away at my clothes and exposed skin.

I sucked in a breath and dug my heels in the dirt, hoping the friction would help as I half jogged, half fell down the mountain. Above me, the sound of voices drifted toward my ears. From the corner of my eye, I noticed Jasper attempting to shift his fall toward one of the leaning trees.

"Try to get some cover, Kid," he ordered.

"Easier said than done," I grumbled.

I was doing everything I could to not lose my balance and snap my neck. Huffing, I tried to steer my body toward a set of large boulders.

Static filled my ear. "Almost at the bottom," Amerie puffed.

As soon as the words left her mouth, I felt a bullet whizz past my ear, whipping my loose hair across my forehead.

No longer caring about controlling my speed, I stopped digging my fingers and heels into the ground and slid toward the boulders. My leg rammed into the top of the grey slab, bouncing me over the side. I felt my heart lodge in my throat as my arms flailed wildly, desperately trying to grasp something.

The cold, jagged edge of the rock sliced into my finger-tips. Flexing my hand, I gripped the edge as hard as I could and felt my body snap as my momentum came to an abrupt stop.

An agonized cry tore from my lips as my shoulder screamed in agony. Ignoring the pain, I reached up with my other hand and pulled my body up and over the boulder. Clenching my teeth so hard it hurt, I wedged my foot between a fallen tree limb and rock to keep from sliding and started returning fire.

Across from me, Jasper laid sprawled on the ground with one leg wrapped around a fallen tree. A large cut ran across his face.

"You good, Kid?"

I gritted my teeth. "Never better."

I lined up a target and fired. My bullet hit the man square in the chest. He lurched forward and crashed down the mountain. Gravel and branches followed his descent.

I ducked my head, just barely dodging a branch about the size of my arm careening toward me. I winced as the jagged edges of my boulder dug into my cheek.

The quick movement caused my foot to slip, and I felt my leg twist as I crashed to the ground.

"This sucks," I mumbled.

My hand wrapped around a smaller rock, providing enough support to help me back up. Another spray of bullets pelted the area around me. Splinters of rock sliced deeper into my already shredded skin.

Grumbling, I lifted my bloody hand back toward my trigger. Just as my sights landed on a target, a sharp burst of flames ignited in my side, knocking me down.

I rolled a few feet and slammed into another boulder. I sucked in a deep breath and tried to breathe slowly out my nose.

Damn, that hurts.

I clutched my side. Blood oozed around my fingers. Clenching my teeth, I packed some dirt in the hole and then reached for my M4 lying next to my feet. I crawled onto my knees and moved my crosshairs onto a new target.

Bullets bounced all around my new location. Grumbling, I pulled my trigger. A man tumbled off the cliff. Swiveling, I lined my sights on the man standing next to him and squeezed. A heartbeat later, he followed his friend down the mountain.

A bullet bounced off the top of my sad excuse of a cover, sending gravel chips on top of my head. Ducking lower, I rolled my eyes. "Great job, Greer…" I lined up another target and fired. "You picked the absolute worst spot to shoot from."

The bullets slowed their assault, allowing me time to assess my area. I almost laughed as I realized what I was going to have to do.

Glancing back at the ridge, I saw a man holding an RPG, aiming at my position.

"Lord, please don't let me break my neck," I prayed as I pushed away from the rock.

My body hung in the air for half a heartbeat and then crashed into the ground. Black spots dotted the edge of my vision as the air rushed out of my lungs. Twisting my body, I started sliding on my backside.

Something grabbed my foot and my body lurched forward, slamming my face into a leaning tree. Blood spurted from my nose, creating a red barrier. Gasping, I wiped away the mess and glanced down at my foot lodged between the tree's roots.

"Shit!"

Desperately, I clawed at the ensnaring hooks, expecting an explosion at any second. When nothing happened, I risked a quick peek over my shoulder.

The man lay crumpled on the ground with the RPG lying next to him. I swiveled my head toward Jasper.

"Thanks."

He nodded. "Hurry up. We need to get off this mountain."

"Working on it," I grumbled as my hands went back to working on the damn roots.

Down below us, bullets started whizzing past us.

You've got to be kidding me.

Static filled my ear. "We've got y'all covered," Dee called out.

Freeing my foot, I began control falling again. "Just don't accidentally hit us."

I could hear Amerie's eye roll. "Hard to miss your big butt."

A smile flitted onto my lips, making my bumpy journey a little more bearable. Movement flashed by, and I watched as Jasper zoomed past me. His movements seemed almost graceful as he steered himself down the mountain.

Furrowing my brow, I tried to mimic his movements, when curses filled my ears.

"Damn it!" Dee yelled.

"They're swarming down here." Amerie cursed, and our covering fire vanished.

Not good.

I spared a quick glance over my shoulder just in time to see another man pick up the fallen RPG.

"Ah hell."

Partially crouching, I half ran, half fell down the mountain. A loud explosion sounded behind me, and then I was launched into the air.

Chapter 24

FOR TWO LONG HEARTBEATS, I JUST SEEMED TO HANG IN THE air. Rocks and tree limbs loomed below me.

This is going to hurt...

As soon as the thought crossed my mind, my body crashed down. The breath was knocked out of my lungs as my shoulder bounced off a rock, causing my body to start somersaulting down.

Green and brown blurbs raced past me.

Tree limbs and sharp rocks clawed at my body and a sticky liquid coated the side of my face. Bouncing off the side of a boulder, a cool blast of air touched my back as I was once again catapulted into the air.

Black spots dotted the edge of my vision as my side hit the ground with a loud thump. Unable to breathe, I tried to grab onto anything to slow my descent.

Roots, rocks, and limbs slid through my sliced hands.

Like a runaway log, my body's momentum only continued to pick up speed. The ground below me disappeared for a second and then came crashing back up at me again.

A cry burst from lips as my side rammed into a tree and then smashed to the level ground.

My vision went black.

"Kid!" Jasper's scream filled my ringing head.

Groaning, I rolled over onto my back. "I'm still alive," I croaked out.

Every bone in my body felt broken.

Wincing, I crawled to my knees.

"I'm on my way, Kid," Amerie called out.

Nodding, I looked around me. Bodies lay strewn across the ground. A trail of blood seeped down into the creek, tainting the water pink.

"I'm still alive," I repeated with more strength. As long as I was still breathing, I could keep fighting.

Movement flashed by. Tilting my head, I glimpsed the barrel of a gun starting to point toward me.

I lurched to my feet and dove behind the closest tree as a bullet raced past my head. I reached behind me to pull my M4 around, but grabbed air.

Crap, crap, crap!

It must have fallen off of me when I fell off the damn mountain. Bullets continued to spray the tree, raining bark and gravel down around me. I reached down to my pant leg where I kept my SIG, but once again my fingers grabbed air. Even my knife had been lost to my fall.

"Great," I mumbled.

I scanned the area around me, checking the bush where I had placed the weapons for the prison soldiers to use. The closest weapon was several yards away.

I looked up to the sky. "I survive that fall only to be stranded weaponless?"

A bullet chipped away next to my ear, causing me to duck lower. I heard a click and then a low grumbling.

Peering around the trunk, I saw a young kid fumbling in his pocket for another magazine. His round eyes met mine and then darted back to his task. Without thinking, I sprinted toward the kid in a low crouch and wrapped my arms around his waist, tackling him to the ground.

He grunted as I threw my fist into his side, knocking the gun from his hands.

The kid shifted beneath me and threw his elbow up, popping my head back. A tangy metallic taste filled my mouth. I threw a quick jab, but my knuckles only grazed his chin as the boy rolled out from under me. Before I could react, the kid's hand rammed into my injured side, stealing the breath from my lungs.

Kicking out, I jammed my foot into his shoulder. He fell forward, allowing me time to crawl out from under him. The boy's long arms whipped out and his fingers dug into the bullet hole in my shoulder.

Pain erupted, and I cried out. Black spots dotted my vision and it was all I could do to keep from passing out. The sound of a snapping branch and approaching footsteps barely registered in my muddled brain before I felt myself lurch upwards. A cold metal blade pressed tightly against my throat.

I struggled against the chokehold and met determined eyes. Seeing Amerie's cold gaze, I ceased my struggles and went limp in the boy's arms.

He gripped me tighter and began yelling at Amerie. I felt the blade bite into my skin, but I forced myself to remain motionless.

A muscle twitched in Amerie's cheek and then she squeezed the trigger. Warm liquid coated the back of my head and ran down onto my neck.

I felt the boy's body slowly slide and crumple to the ground. The knife he held nicked my skin, causing a small trickle of blood to run down my throat.

I placed my hand over the cut and took a ragged inhale. "Thanks," I huffed.

Amerie walked up next to me. Her gaze drifted over my bruised and swollen face, down to my shoulder, before stopping on my still bleeding side wound. "You look like shit."

Snorting, I met her gaze. "You don't look so hot yourself."

Blood soaked her pant leg and her face looked like it had barely survived an attack from an angry mountain lion. Looking down at the ground, she shook her head and chuckled. When she met my gaze again, the humor in her eyes shifted to something more serious.

"Seriously, though, you okay?"

I nodded and gazed at her thigh. "Yeah, you?"

"Nothing a little dirt can't fix."

She glanced down at the dead soldier and winced. "He's just a kid…can't be more than sixteen." She sighed.

I nudged her with my good shoulder. "A kid who would have killed me and you if he had the chance." I knelt and took the kid's extra rounds. "You didn't kill him. His government did."

She took a deep breath and nodded. She reached behind her and handed my M4 to me. "Found this thing hanging from a tree limb back there." Her eyes filled with a humorous twinkle. "Guess it's your lucky day."

I snorted as I grabbed extra clips from the other dead soldiers. "Yeah, I'm planning on buying a lottery ticket after this," I quipped in my most deadpan voice.

A strangled noise came from Amerie. She bit her lip, but the sound escaped into a belly-grabbing laugh.

Hearing her deep cackles halted my movements. "It wasn't that funny." Concern tainted my words. Was she going into shock?

Wiping tears from her eyes, she straightened back up. "Can you just imagine?" Another snicker escaped. "Us? Winning the lottery?"

My mouth opened, but no words came out as she giggled some more. Before I could question her sanity, a rustle in the trees grabbed our attention.

Crouching low, we trained our muzzles on the incoming sound.

The rustling ceased.

We waited a few seconds and then the soft sounds of movement started back up again. I looked through my scope, searching for the threat.

"To the right," Amerie whispered as she slowly stood up.

I rotated to the right and saw a blue jay perched on the edge of a tree branch. Smiling, I rocked back on my heels and watched the bird. "Hey, Angelette."

Amerie cocked an eyebrow at me. "How hard did you hit your head?"

I rolled my eyes. She wanted to question *my* lucidity?

"They say blue jays are angels visiting from heaven."

Amerie shifted her gaze from me to the blue jay watching us. "Well, Angelette, we could use all the help we can get." Taking a quick look at her watch, she began walking through the trees. "We've only got twenty minutes to get out of here."

I felt my forehead wrinkle as the blue jay flew away. "Twenty minutes till the airstrike?"

Amerie's gaze zoomed in on my forehead. "I think you hit that noggin of yours really hard." She smirked at my unamused expression. "Did you not hear Bookie earlier?"

My feet faltered as I stared blankly at her. "No, I was a little busy falling down the side of a mountain."

Amerie's mouth hung open as she gave a slow thoughtful

nod. "Oh, yeah." She frowned. "About that, you weren't very graceful. I expected more from you."

I scowled at her. "What did Bookie say, smartass?"

Amerie slowed her pace, her expression becoming more serious. I scanned the area as the sound of gunfire and the scent of cordite overwhelmed my senses.

"Bookie got the warehouse coordinates to Washington. They agreed to an immediate attack." Amerie looked back and met my gaze. "That was over two hours ago."

Nodding, I moved my finger closer to my trigger. "So, twenty minutes."

Amerie wriggled her eyebrows. "Guess we'd better hurry up...I'd hate to find out what happens if we don't reach that safety zone Sheba and Hollywood marked."

I smirked. "I can tell...I know you aren't running just for the exercise."

Amerie rolled her eyes, causing my smirk to grow. We both picked up the pace and jogged as fast as our battered bodies would carry us. Overhead, the sun's rays danced across the red snow. Cordite and smoke hovered in the air, making it difficult to breathe. Gunfire and shouts became more distinguishable as the tree line began to thin.

Static filled my ears. "Kid. Legacy. Location?" Emersyn's voice muffled my labored breathing.

"About to join the party," Amerie panted.

We slowed our movements as the battle sounds became amplified. My finger hovered over the trigger as we slinked closer to the edge of the tree line.

"Good. Time's running out," Emersyn stated in a breathless voice.

A layer of smoke hovered over the area. Bodies lay scattered over the well-trodden path.

My gaze traveled over the motionless figures to a small

group forming an arch. Mixed in with skinny soldiers dressed in rags, I caught sight of the rest of my dysfunctional family, firing relentlessly at the swarming ants. They formed a strong front, preventing the Koreans from pushing forward.

I turned my attention back to the field and slowed when I saw the motionless figures dressed in dirty rags. My stomach knotted at the sight of the dead prisoners. They were so close to home.

The thought of these poor men never seeing their families again caused bile to fill in my mouth. Movement flashed in the edge of my vision. Kneeling down, I peered through my scope and saw Clark crawling toward the trees.

I sucked in a breath.

A bloody hand clutched his stomach as he inched away from the flying bullets. His face was scrunched in pain, but the determined glint in his eyes said he'd make it to the tree line.

Amerie crouched low beside me. "We sneak through these trees and then, with cover, we should be able to make it to the safety zone." A smile pulled at her lips. "And then we can use the remaining few minutes to shoot those assholes for all the pain they have caused."

When I didn't smile back, she frowned. Her head swiveled to follow the direction of my gaze.

"Clark!" She gasped as she lunged toward him.

I quickly grabbed her arm and pulled her back.

"Let me go! They're going to kill him. I have to help him before the airstrike happens."

The glint in her eyes said she was a few seconds away from punching me in the face.

"Stand down, Anderson," I ordered. I gave her a small shove and ignored her narrowed gaze. "You go running in there, you're just going to get yourself and Clark killed."

She huffed but nodded.

I pointed at the set of trees Clark was trying to reach. "Go in from there while I provide you both cover. From there, follow your original plan to get to the safety zone."

Amerie held my gaze. "And you?"

I broke eye contact as I lowered my body to the ground for better stability.

"You're not going to have enough time to run through the trees…" Amerie whispered.

I nodded. "You'd better provide me some great cover." I held her gaze and smirked. "I really don't want to be shot in the back while I run to the safety zone."

Amerie took a deep breath and nodded.

I lined Clark in my scope as Amerie took off sprinting. I shifted my sights to two men shooting near Clark and lined my crosshairs in the center of one man's chest.

Aim small, miss small.

I squeezed the trigger and watched as he fell lifelessly into the snow. Shifting a few inches over, I dropped the other man before he could even turn.

"Kid, what the hell are you still doing over there?" Jasper yelled.

I winced as my eardrums rang with his angry voice.

Bullets sprayed the tree above me.

"Providing cover for Legacy and Clark," I answered as another man found his way into my sights. I heard Jasper yell at someone to assist Amerie, followed by the low roar of the approaching air strike.

Not good…

The Koreans seemed to pause as some of them turned their eyes toward the sky. Using their distraction to my advantage, I threw out a can of smoke and watched as the surrounding area filled with the thick fog.

Waiting for cover, I let the smoke billow up and lined a couple more targets in my crosshairs.

"You'd better go now, Kid," Jasper ordered.

Inhaling deeply, I pushed to my feet and bounded into the clearing. "Don't shoot me," I pleaded as I began sprinting as fast as I could.

Bullets whizzed past me as I ran. I kept my head low and pumped my legs as hard and fast as I could, dodging fallen bodies and scattered weapons as I went.

Jasper's tense voice urged me to run faster. Even from my distance, I couldn't miss the worried expression on his tight face.

"Hundred yards…you got this. Hundred yards, come on, Greer," I mumbled breathlessly.

My legs burned and my bruised ribcage made it difficult to keep going, but I pushed through the pain. Overhead, the approaching bomber blocked out all other noises.

Adrenaline and pure terror pumped energy into my weary and broken body. Through the haze, I saw Amerie join Jasper's side. It was hard to tell, but it looked like a flash of horror sparked across her face. I watched as she raised her gun and then a piercing shot filled my ears.

A searing pain erupted near my knee. My legs buckled, and I slammed head first into the cold ground. A shadow zoomed over me as I rolled over to my back.

Breathless, it took me several shaky breaths to realize the shadow belonged to the bomber.

"Kid!" Emersyn's sharp tone pierced through my pain.

Rolling to my stomach, I saw her tiny form racing toward me. Something inside told me I needed to move.

Moaning, I slowly rose to my feet. A muffled cry tore from my lips as I forced myself to put weight on my leg. Ignoring the pain, I hobbled toward Emersyn. Behind her, I could see Dee and Sterling firing at the men still shooting at us, while Evan and Parker helped the wounded to safety.

Sweat ran down my bloody face and black spots dotted my vision. Over my labored breathing I heard a low whistle block out all other sounds.

I'm not going to make it.

A wall of heat erupted behind me and I was catapulted into the air and then slammed into the ground. Blackness engulfed me, and I struggled to breathe.

Buzzing filled my ears.

Slowly, I peeled my eyes open. I tilted my head to the side and saw Emersyn's small form crawling toward me. I wriggled my arm and felt a sticky liquid covering my fingers. I followed the red trail down to a huge puddle surrounding my leg.

My forehead scrunched up just as Emersyn reached my side. Her round eyes traveled over my body.

"Doc!" she yelled. "Doc, get over here now!"

Her voice sounded like she was underwater. I wanted to tell her it was way too cold to be swimming right now, but the thought of just speaking made me tired.

That's what I need…a nap. A nice, long nap…

A shadow fell over me. "Stay awake, Greer," Evan ordered, his tone sharp.

A searing pain bit into my thigh. My eyes popped open to see what was trying to cut my leg off. Evan's big hands left my thigh, but a constricting strap wrapped tightly around my skin remained.

A small whimper left my lips and I felt myself being lifted up.

"She needs an evac now," Evan said to someone over a deafening whooshing sound.

I rolled my head to the side and searched for the source of

the strange sound. Dust billowed around us and clawed at my face, forcing me to turn my head away from it.

Out of the corner of my eye, I saw a flash of blue. My lips tipped up when I recognized the blue jay Amerie and I had seen earlier.

"Angelette," I whispered.

The bird floated to a nearby branch and stared at me. Its dark eyes bored into mine and I felt an overwhelming sadness wash over me.

The darkness tugged at my eyelids, but I fought its pull.

The bird raised its wings and launched off into the air.

Panic filled me. I wasn't ready for Angelette to leave.

I missed my friend.

I wanted to talk to her.

"Wait," I whispered.

Black spots dotted my vision.

The bird swooped to the ground and then rose back in a graceful arch before disappearing into the trees. A muffled cry escaped my lips.

"Please come back," I pleaded. "Angelette, I'm—"

Chapter 25

ROUND, GREEN EYES STARED BACK AT ME AS DARKNESS wrapped me in its embrace.

Uneasiness trickled down my spine as I registered the fear gazing back at me. I blinked, trying to recall where I was and how I had fallen into the black pit, but a thick haze kept my memories at bay.

My heart started to pick up its pace, and I struggled to breathe.

Clipped male voices spoke above me. "Vitals are dropping."

I heard a sharp inhale mix in with a slow, uneven beeping.

"Legacy, did we make a mistake pushing to have her transported?" a Southern female's voice whispered thickly.

The green eyes—Legacy's—pooled with tears. "They didn't have the proper equipment there. At least this way she stood a chance."

I watched the tears roll down her face as a loud, drawn-out beep pierced my ears.

"Clear," a male voice said.

Electricity buzzed around my head, followed by a surge jolting through my body. My eyes slammed shut, and the worried green eyes were replaced by another set of green eyes.

No fear or sorrow tainted these eyes. Instead, happiness gazed down at me.

A calming sensation cascaded through my body.

Angelette.

I wanted to say something, but the unrelenting, long, flat tone made it impossible to concentrate.

Another surge jerked my body violently, and my vision flickered back to the scared green eyes. Tears ran freely down her face.

Another shock convulsed my body.

I took one last look at the fear-filled eyes before gazing back into Angelette's happier ones.

Darkness and silence surrounded me.

Where am I?

A sick feeling settled at the bottom of my stomach. I had no idea where *this* was, but deep down, I knew it wasn't where I wanted to be.

Pushing against the heavy weight that pressed down on my body, a buzzing sound gradually began to fill my ears. The noise grew to an annoyingly loud mixture of humming machines and different voices.

"Cerebral edema…"

"Several fractured ribs…"

"Stopped the bleeding…"

"Not sure we'll be able to save it…"

My heart began to beat faster. Before the panic could overwhelm me, something warm grabbed my hand.

"It's going to take a lot more than feistiness and grit to beat this, Greer," a male voice whispered in my ear.

An image of a man with light brown hair popped into my mind, but before I could recognize his face, the image disappeared.

Something in the man's tone made me want to call him a pain in the ass, but when I tried to voice my thoughts, my lips refused to work.

My heartbeat shot off as the panic returned.

Blaring alarms erupted around me, and all of the voices started shouting. Their words pounded into my skull and shattered my eardrums. My chest constricted tightly, squeezing the air from my lungs.

Something pressed down hard against my mouth. I tried to yell at the voices and let them know they were suffocating me, but only my hearing seemed to be functioning.

"I can't breathe!" I screamed silently. *"I can't brea—"*

"SHEBA, I'M SCARED," a soft woman's voice murmured in the darkness.

"Me too, Legacy…me too," Sheba, I assumed, whispered in a barely audible voice.

Someone took a deep breath.

"I've never been a religious person," Legacy stated. "With everything we've seen and had to do…I just found it hard to believe in anything. But when we…" she stopped and cleared her throat, "…when we were transferring from the hospital in China to here in Germany, and Kid almost—" Legacy's voice caught.

Several seconds of silence passed before she started speaking again. "I prayed. I've never done that before. What if it doesn't work? What if she—"

"Hey," Sheba cut her off in a firm, yet gentle voice. "I'll never judge whether you choose to have faith or not. Honestly, it's human to have questions and to doubt, but don't lose your faith in Kid. She's a fighter. She *will* pull through this."

I had no idea who these two women were, but I found myself relaxed by their presence. And although I remained imprisoned in the darkness's embrace, I felt safe knowing they were here with me.

A door creaked open, followed by an irritating, high-pitched voice. "Only family and staff are allowed in this room."

I heard teeth grinding above my head. For some reason, I found myself looking forward to Legacy's response, but Sheba's Southern voice quickly replied, "We're her sisters."

The irritating woman huffed. "You cannot be in here. You will leave this room."

"Like hell we will," Legacy shot back.

If I hadn't been a captive to the darkness, I would have busted out laughing. I could picture the irritating woman's jaw dropping from Legacy's blatant refusal.

Before the woman could respond, the door opened and a man's deep voice spoke up. "Miss Anderson, you are non-weight bearing. You and Miss Brooks need to sit down."

Low mumbles and shuffled footsteps filled the silence.

"Now, what is the problem?" the man asked.

"Dr. Tarrant, I told them only family and staff were allowed in the room," the irritating woman whined.

Legacy grumbled low under her breath. I wasn't positive, but I could have sworn she called the woman a snitch.

"I can see the family resemblance. Can't you?" the man's tone made me want to smile.

I liked this man.

The irritating woman sputtered.

"I'll take care of this," the man said, effectively dismissing the woman.

Low snickers filled my ears as a door closed shut.

"Oh, stop scowling, Knoxy," Legacy goaded. I could hear the eye roll she gave him.

"Legacy, if I see you put weight on that leg again, I will find a way to chain you to that wheelchair," the man threatened. "Both of your bodies have gone through a serious ordeal and they need time to heal. You are not doing your sister any favors by not taking care of yourselves."

A shot of fear coursed through me.

I didn't understand why I felt so protective over these two women, but hearing they were hurt scared me more than being trapped by the darkness.

Completely unfazed by the man's tone, Legacy ignored his scolding. "How is she?"

It took the man several minutes to answer.

"On paper, it doesn't look good." A slightly amused pitch entered his tone. "But having the odds stacked against Greer has never stopped her before. She's a fighter, and she needs to be reminded of that every day."

"She can hear us?" Sheba asked.

"Not all coma patients show signs they can hear and understand what is going on around them, but if I had to bet money, I'd say Greer is listening to every word we say right now."

Legacy chuckled. "I bet she was laughing and rolling her eyes at our little confrontation with that nurse."

Something warm brushed against my head.

"Did y'all get rid of all of her weapons?" Legacy whispered in a mocking tone.

"Most coma patients have no need for an M4," the man answered slowly.

"Good, because when she finds out you shaved some of

her hair off, she will shoot you where it hurts." Legacy sounded way too chipper by the thought.

For some reason, anger ignited within me. I felt the need to punch the man, but I had no idea why.

The man laughed. "Good to know. I'll keep that in mind." His serious tone returned. "As entertaining as this has been, visitation is over for tonight. Greer needs her rest and so do you two."

The two women grumbled but did as they were told.

Something warm grabbed my hand.

"Dr. Pain-in-the-Ass says you can hear everything we're saying to you…so stop being a little drama queen and wake up already," Legacy ordered.

Before I could think of some smartass retort, liquid splashed against my skin.

"Please," Legacy choked out. "I need my sister."

Don't be sad.

I struggled against the darkness, desperate to break free. I didn't understand why, but I knew I caused Legacy's tears, and I hated it.

As I fought the darkness's restraints, I heard the door open and close.

Silence swooped in, suffocating me.

I felt alone.

Weak.

The darkness began to pull at my eyelids. Just as I began to lose consciousness, I heard something scrape across the floor. Warmth engulfed my hand, keeping the darkness at bay.

The man released a weary sigh, and for the first time, I heard the exhaustion in his voice.

"I never told you this during training, but I knew you had everything it took to become a SEAL the moment you put your hands on your hips and glared defiantly at me." The man chuckled softly. "When I saw that spark in your eyes, I knew there was something special about you."

His words felt familiar, but I had no idea why.

"And you showed me," he said with a snort. "The way you refused to back down and literally give everything you had to pass PST…I loved seeing that fight in you."

He was quiet for several minutes.

So soft, I barely heard him, he whispered, "If I tell you you can't do this, you'll probably bounce right up with a snarky comment just to spite me."

I felt a brief moment of humor spark within me, followed by a gentle hand squeeze.

"You can't do this. You're too small, too fragile to wake up. There is no way you can beat this. You will fail."

Anger surged through me.

Who did this man think he was? I wanted to snap at him and tell him he had *no* idea what I was capable of doing.

Beeping filled my ears as I struggled against the darkness. The black restraints clung tightly to my body, but I could tell their hold was weakening.

"Keep fighting, Greer," the man urged.

Fatigue started to weigh my body down. Ignoring my muscles' plea to rest, I fought harder to move, but it felt as if I had been thrown into a pool of drying cement. The darkness danced around the corners of my vision, threatening to pull me back under.

Come on, Greer!

I did not want to get sucked back. What I wanted was to flip the darkness off…and I would if my arms ever decided to work.

Using every ounce of strength I had, I forced my eyes to open.

Familiar dark blue eyes stared down at me.

A smile spread across the man's face and his mouth moved, but I couldn't hear what he said. I opened my mouth to tell him, but pain erupted. Something pressed against my face, keeping my mouth from moving.

Panic spread throughout me. The sound of my racing heartbeats threatened to explode my eardrums. Movement flashed by and I had the feeling more people had entered the room.

A warm sensation flowed through my system, forcing the panic away. Exhaustion swept through me, and I knew the darkness was going to come back. Just before it engulfed me in its embrace again, I locked eyes with the man.

Knox.

Chapter 26

SOFT MURMURS DRIFTED OVER ME, GENTLY PULLING ME BACK to the light. Something eased through my hair, instantly calming me. My mind drifted back to when I was little and my mom would play with my hair.

"When you look good, you feel good, when you feel good, you do good," a woman said in a thick Cajun voice.

"Well, Granny, I know what will really make her feel good," Amerie stated.

My lips twitched, hearing Amerie's distant voice. The soft melody of *Bad Company* drifted down to me. My lips twitched again as I pictured Amerie getting into the song.

"Look!" Dee exclaimed. "Her lips just moved. I think she's smiling."

"Told you this would work," Amerie said in a smug voice.

I wanted to open my eyes so badly, but for some reason, they refused to work. The gentle tug on my hair vanished, and a strong scent of perfume flooded my senses.

"She looks a lot better now that Knoxy got rid of those tubes covering her face."

Shuffled footsteps moved toward me. A fluffy material wrapped around my hand. "Knox said she was breathing good on her own." Emersyn's proud voice drifted down to me.

I tried again to open my eyes.

"Look, her eyes fluttered."

I could hear the smile in Emersyn's voice. I felt rather than heard the others move in closer. Their presence gave me strength, and I tried again to pry open my eyes.

Nothing.

A weight pressed down on them, but I kept pushing. I felt like I should be covered in sweat, but still I forced my body to keep trying.

Beeping began to fill up the room.

Quick, purposeful footsteps marched in.

"Alright, visitation time is over for the day," a deep voice ordered.

Grumbles sounded and then the warm sensation crept back into my body.

No!

I struggled against the pull. I didn't want to sleep anymore. I wanted to see my friends.

"Way to go, Knoxy, you pissed her off."

Even in my muddled state I couldn't miss the pleased tone in Amerie's voice.

A deep chuckle pierced through the darkness. "It wouldn't be the first time."

MACHINES HUMMED all around me when my eyes finally opened. A warm hand grasped mine. I followed the hand up to a head lying down on my mattress.

"Mom?" I croaked.

The sunlight streaming through the window blinds created dancing shadows over her furrowed brow. Using my finger, I gently smoothed out the stress lines, knowing I was to blame for putting them there.

A shadow passed over her body as the door creaked open, blocking out the small rays of sunlight.

Dad walked in with a cup of coffee. "They are serving breakfast if you—"

His mouth dropped. "Greer." He rushed forward and cupped my face. His movements jostled Mom from her sleep, and she turned dazed eyes toward me.

"Greer Martha," she gasped, wrapping her arms tightly around me.

A smile stretched across my face, causing my cheek muscles to ache, but I didn't care. For the first time in a long time, I felt safe.

Liquid dripped on my cheek, and I tilted my head up to see silent tears running down Mom's face.

"Don't cry, Mom," I croaked out. I tried to clear my throat to make my voice louder, but my mouth was so dry it didn't make a difference.

She wiped away the fallen tears with the back of her hand. "I'm not crying." She gave a small laugh. "I'm just so happy to see you awake."

Dad released me and stepped back. A smile spread across his scruffy face that hadn't been shaved for several days. "How do you feel?"

Before I could answer, my door opened again and in walked a tall man with light brown hair. "Is everything okay? I saw the call light?"

I peered around Mom and saw dark blue eyes gazing down at me. I felt my lips start to curve up as I recognized the familiar face.

"Knox?"

A crooked grin lit his face up. "Looks like someone finally decided to wake up."

Finally?

I frowned, my eyebrows pulling together. "How long was I out?"

Mom and Dad exchanged a look before answering. "You've been in a coma for two weeks."

My mouth dropped.

What had happened while I was out? Did we succeed? Did my sisters make it out?

I gasped. "My sisters? Are they okay? Where are the boys? How is everyone?"

Knox raised a hand to silence the torrent of questions pouring from my mouth. "Slow down," he said with a chuckle. "Everyone is fine. They've all been worried about you. You receive more visitors than all of our patients here." Knox looked over his shoulder. "I'm surprised they haven't come running in here yet."

I smiled. I had no doubt my sisters had given him heck while I was trapped in the coma.

"Can I see them?"

Knox's eyes twinkled. "You can't go anywhere, but they can come visit you for a little bit." His gaze drifted over the machines before glancing back at me. "Is there anything else you need? Anything hurting?"

I shook my head. "I just need to see my friends."

Smiling, Knox nodded and walked from the room.

Dad used the controls and adjusted my bed so that I was in a sitting position.

I beamed at him. "Thanks."

A commotion sounded in the hallway, and before I knew what was going on, three wheelchairs zoomed into my room.

"Kid!" Amerie rolled to my side with a broad grin stretched across her face.

Dee and Emersyn followed closely behind her. Before I could even utter a sound, the Brits squeezed into the packed space, and some adults I didn't recognize hovered around my door.

I watched silently as the Brits shuffled toward the end of my bed. They each had small unhealed cuts and light bruises marking their faces. Sterling and Jasper appeared to be in the worst shape, with Sterling's arm in a cast and Jasper hobbling on crutches.

I swiveled my head to the side of my bed where my sisters were. Amerie's left eye had a light green tint on the lower corner and she sported a scabbed lip. Her leg was propped up with several rods and screws embedded in her skin.

Emersyn's face seemed to have healed the best since the attack, but her arms were wrapped in thick white bandages that smelled an awful lot like fish.

My gaze fell on Dee last. As I took in her dolled-up face, I couldn't help but smile. It looked like she had a deep gash above her eye, but the foundation she wore made it look more like a scratch. My gaze traveled down to the back brace she wore before stopping on her arm in a sling.

I glanced over the large group and smiled. "Hey."

"About time you woke your lazy ass up," Amerie teased.

I chuckled. "Missed you too, Legacy."

Standing by the door, a woman in dark jeans and a fringed coat shook her head. "Merie-Lou," she chastised. Meeting my gaze, she frowned. "I tried to teach Amerie she can think what she wants, but she doesn't have to say it."

I laughed. "We've tried to teach her the same thing."

Behind the woman, the rest of my sister's family chuckled. I tilted my head to get a glimpse at all of their faces, but some of my hair fell in front of my eyes, blocking my vision. My forehead wrinkled as I reached up and pushed it aside.

That's not how I part my hair.

I ran my fingers through the new part. Amerie slid a glance toward Knox, standing next to her mom, and smirked. A sinking feeling settled in my stomach. I moved my hair back to my old part and brushed against a prickly patch.

No…

Gasping, I ran my hands over the patch several more times before glaring at Knox.

"You. Cut. My. Hair."

Amerie snickered and mumbled something about taking my guns away, while Knox actually managed to look a little contrite.

"It had to be done. You had…"

I tuned him out as he explained why and how important it was to shave part of my head. I didn't want to hear it. I didn't care.

An elderly woman with bright red lipstick and beaded necklaces pushed forward to my bed. I breathed in her perfume as she smiled warmly at me. "Don't you worry none, child. Granny styled it just right."

Dee nodded. "You can't even tell."

I smiled at Granny. She shared the same mischievous smile as Dee. She stuck out her wrinkled hand and grasped mine.

"It's so good to see you awake," she said as she patted my hand tenderly.

I instantly liked the woman. She had a spark in her that couldn't be dimmed.

As she pulled her hand back, I noticed an old leather watch that looked very familiar. She caught my stare and winked. At the end of my bed, Sterling stared wistfully at it.

Granny's eyes sparked with mischief. "Those British gentlemen are such sweet boys, but they play cards about as good as my Davine."

Amerie snorted while both Dee and Sterling frowned.

"Granny, you don't really plan on keeping that, do you?" Dee asked. "It doesn't match any of your outfits."

Granny gave me a wink before turning toward Dee. "I won this watch fair and square. Of course I'm keeping it." She placed a hand on her hip and waved a bright-red mani-cured finger at the Brits. "Someone has to teach those boys how dangerous it is to play the devil's game."

Dee's mouth dropped. "Granny, you go gambling all the time."

Chuckles filled my room as Granny shrugged her shoulders. "I'm nearly ninety-five years old. I'm allowed to have fun with the devil every now and then."

I laughed until my cheeks started to ache. Leaning against my pillow, I tried and failed to suppress a yawn. I couldn't believe after basically two weeks of sleeping, I could possibly be tired, but my eyelids began to droop.

Knox stepped forward. "Alright, visitation time is over."

"No," I rushed out. "I'm fine."

When he started to shake his head, I added a soft, "Please?"

Knox huffed. "You have five minutes with your team, and then I'm kicking everyone out."

My welcoming committee slowly trickled out of the room with soft goodbyes and small waves. Just before Knox followed behind my parents, he stopped in the doorway and gave me a pointed stare.

He held up his hand. "Five minutes."

"Knoxy, where's the trust?" Amerie feigned a hurt tone. "Do you really think we'd ignore your order?"

The corner of Knox's lips lifted as he shook his head and walked out. I waited until Amerie turned back to face me before I arched an eyebrow.

"Knoxy?"

Sterling snorted. "She's given every patient and staff member here a nickname."

Resisting the urge to laugh, I narrowed my gaze at Amerie. "Do I even want to know about all of the trouble you managed to get in while I was out?"

"I've been a perfect angel." The innocent look she wore only lasted a second before a wicked glint entered her eyes. "Do you remember anything from these past two weeks? Knox said there was a chance you could hear us."

My forehead wrinkled. I tried to recall something, anything, but gave up when my head started to throb.

"Honestly, it feels like we were on the mountain yesterday."

Images of Amerie and me running toward the safe zone flashed in my mind. I could smell the thick layer of cordite in the air and see the motionless men scattered across the ground. I remembered one crawling—

I gasped. "Clark! Your brother, is he okay?"

Amerie nodded, instantly calming me down. "He's fine. He would have been among your entourage but he's in physical therapy."

"Physical therapy?" I asked.

Amerie dropped my gaze and swallowed. "He's paralyzed from the waist down." Chuckling softly, she looked up. "Not that he's letting it slow him down any. He's already looking into the Paralympics."

I smiled. "Good." My mind wandered to the fallen men from the prison camp. "How many did we lose?"

"Seven," Evan answered. "Four Americans and three British."

"Things were pretty hectic after the blast," Parker said. "A group of Apaches took out most of the remaining Koreans on the ground while rescue helos came and got the critically wounded."

A wicked grin curved his lips. "Special Forces from the U.S. and Britain dropped in and helped finish the job. Marines have been going in and out of North Korea since then. They took the capital the other day. The North Korean leader is now on the run."

I leaned back into my pillow and smiled.

We did it.

"That's not the only good news," Dee chimed in. "Since the New York attack, a lot of volunteers enlisted. We now have the numbers we need to be a threat in this war."

"Amazing what happens when we work together instead of fighting against one another," Emersyn quipped.

"Don't forget to tell her about our sisters from Team Two kicking some major ass in Russia," Amerie boasted. "I hear if we keep this up, the war will be over before we know it."

"Wow!" I chuckled. "I've missed a lot."

Before anyone could respond, someone knocked on my door.

That can't be five minutes already.

I started to protest but stopped when I recognized the familiar crooked smile that leaned in.

"I heard our Sleeping Beauty finally decided to wake up." John walked into the room, smiling at me. "You gave us quite the scare, love."

I snorted. "Hey, Casanova."

He patted my hand tenderly before scowling at Evan. "You were supposed to come get me when she woke up."

Evan shrugged. "I guess it slipped my mind."

John's mouth dropped. "That's a horrible thing to say in front of a coma patient." He turned toward me with round, sincere eyes. "Please ignore my rude brother. He has absolutely no couth." He wriggled his eyebrows at my sisters and me. "Especially around gorgeous women."

Laughing, I rolled my eyes. "Your lines are worse than your singing."

John scoffed. "My singing is beautiful."

Shaking my head, I laughed weakly. My eyelids started to droop, but I fought against the pull.

Jasper cleared his throat. "We'll let you rest, Kid."

"I'm—"

He cut me off. "No. You're barely keeping your eyes open. Spend your last few minutes with your sisters. We'll see you tomorrow."

Before I could protest, he hobbled to the side of my bed and gave me a quick hug.

"It's good to have you back," he whispered thickly.

Stunned by the emotion in his voice, I opened and closed my mouth, but no words came out as I gaped at him. Dark shadows rimmed his eyes, and his beard had grown thicker, unrulier.

This was the most unkempt I had ever seen Jasper, and I hated it. Desperate to wash away the stress I had caused, I wracked my brain for something to cheer him up.

"Your wife should have had your son by now. What did y'all name him?" I gave Sterling a sly look. "Please tell me you didn't go with Joker's suggestion."

Jasper's eyes lit up with pure joy, causing my own smile to break free. "Wyatt Reese."

Sterling rolled his eyes. "The only reason he went with your suggestion is because you cheated."

I laughed as he swooped in to give me a hug.

"Cheated?"

He nodded. "You knew I had the most awesome name, so you had to go and jump off that mountain to get the sympathy vote."

"Well damn," I snickered. "I can't get anything past you, Joker."

He winked at me as Parker and then Evan each gave me a hug goodbye, promising to come see me in the morning. I watched as the Brits eased out of my room before turning back toward my sisters.

For several seconds, none of us said anything.

We didn't need to.

After everything we went through, just being with one another was more than enough. My gaze swept over Amerie's healing face, to Dee's back brace, before finally resting on Emersyn's arms covered in white bandages. The longer I focused on the bandages, the more I started smelling fish again.

"Bookie, is there a reason you smell like fish?" I asked.

Amerie laughed. "That's because she's part fish now."

My forehead wrinkled.

Images of running toward the safety zone flashed in my mind. I remembered the burning sting from the bullet and could see Emersyn's wide eyes as she ran toward me just before the explosion.

I glanced back down at the bandages wrapped around her arms. "The blast burned you."

She nodded. Slowly, she unwrapped her bandages, revealing green and brown scales covering her arms. "The doctors layered fish scales to help heal my burns and prevent as much scaring as possible." She glanced down at them. "The cool scales keep most of the pain away, so I guess it's working," she said in a slightly skeptical voice.

Amerie wriggled her eyebrows. "Maybe now since you're half fish, you'll be able to actually keep up with me in the water." She turned toward Dee with a wicked glint in her eye. "Sheba, maybe you should put some on your arms, you might actually beat me."

Emersyn wriggled her arm toward Dee, making her flinch.

Her eyes grew round. "Don't you dare touch me, Bookie. I hate fish. They're icky and slimy and ugh." She shuddered. "There aren't enough bath bombs in the world to wash all of that crud off."

I threw my head back into my pillow and laughed. For someone so tough, Dee could be such a girly-girl.

Emersyn shook her head and twisted her arm to look at her wing tattoo. "You know what the crazy thing is?"

Still chuckling, I arched an eyebrow at her.

"The only parts of my arms that didn't get burned were my two tattoos."

"Wow, that's…"

"Insane? Incredible?" she finished for me.

Nodding, I thought about the wall of heat that had launched me into the air. I didn't feel any discomfort lying down, but I was also fairly certain I was doped up on some high pain meds.

Dee saw the question in my eyes and shook her head. "You didn't get a single burn. It's nothing less than a miracle."

Amerie snorted. "Or more like she was too short for the flames to reach her."

Dee and Amerie shared a quick look that made

Amerie's smirk vanish. I narrowed my gaze at the two of them, but before I could call them out on their weird behavior, Amerie cleared her throat and adopted a more serious tone.

"Pops has been here since we landed in Germany, but he had to leave this morning." Amerie frowned. "We've all been medically discharged."

My mouth dropped. "Really?"

Emersyn snorted. "You're seriously surprised?" She waved a hand at Amerie. "We were all shot numerous times. Legacy broke three ribs and shattered her tibia and femur. My arms and torso are covered in third-degree burns, and Sheba broke four vertebrae and dislocated her shoulder." She turned her gaze toward me. "And you…" She cut off abruptly and averted her gaze.

"And I what?"

No one said anything.

An uneasy feeling trickled down my spine

Before I could demand one of them to tell me what was going on, my parents, Knox, and a blonde nurse strolled into my room.

"Time's up," Knox stated.

I ignored him and kept my gaze locked on my sisters.

Amerie grabbed my hand. "Get some rest."

I arched an eyebrow. "I must be in pretty bad shape if you're willing to run out without a single protest."

Amerie grimaced. "Well, you did try to die on us a few times."

Emersyn gently pushed Amerie out of the way and gave me a quick hug. "So glad you're up and okay."

Dee beamed at me. "Things have been really boring without you."

The blonde nurse standing behind Knox huffed. Dee and

Amerie exchanged knowing smiles. Even Knox struggled to keep an expressionless face.

"Something tells me *that's* not entirely true."

Amerie laughed. "Well, we might have needed a few distractions while your lazy butt slept." She shrugged and swallowed thickly. "You were out for a pretty long time."

She tried to hide the emotion from her voice, but I still heard it. A sharp pain sliced through my chest, knowing I had caused everyone so much worry and grief.

Smirking, I tried to lighten the heavy mood that now weighed the room down. "Can you blame a girl?" I gave her a pointed look. "Your loud mouth would make anyone want to sleep for two weeks."

Chuckles filled the room as Knox ushered the girls out. When the door closed behind them, he turned and faced me. He opened his mouth but stopped when he noticed my narrowed gaze.

"Dr. Pain-in-the-Ass…" There was no way I was going to let him off the hook for shaving my hair. I didn't care about his reasons why or that it was just a small section you couldn't see. Asshole still cut my hair.

Mom gasped. "Greer Martha!"

I ducked my head at her tone. I had heard it enough times when I was younger to know better than to push my luck right now. She was in *serious mode*.

Knox chuckled. "Its fine, Mrs. Connally," he assured while his eyes danced with mischief. "Inside joke." He walked toward the side of my bed and checked the monitors surrounding me. "Do you feel any pain or discomfort?" His gaze met mine, and he pinned me with a pointed look. "Don't act tough. If anything is hurting, you need to let me or a nurse know. Your body does not need to exert itself right now. It needs to heal."

Leaning back against my pillow, I nodded. "I feel fine."

"Greer."

I turned my head to see Mom and Dad staring at me with folded arms.

My lips curved up. "Never could hide anything from y'all." Sighing, I turned my head back toward Knox. "It's not really hurting, it just feels weird."

Knox nodded. "What does?"

I pointed toward my leg. "It itches. And, like, tingles. Kind of like when your foot goes to sleep." I shrugged. "It's uncomfortable, but nothing unbearable."

From the corner of my eye, I noticed my parents exchanged guarded looks as Dad grabbed Mom's hand. Even Knox shifted uncomfortably.

My hand shot up to my head, searching for something else wrong up there. "What are you not telling me?" I gave him a hard stare. If he did anything else to my hair, I was going to find a gun.

Knox sighed. "I didn't want to tell you right away."

"Tell me what?"

He pressed his lips together. "There's no gentle way to say this, Greer." His eyes locked onto mine, knocking the air from my lungs. "We had to amputate your right leg."

My mouth dropped.

It couldn't be.

I ripped the bed sheet back and just gapped at the bandage on my right leg. The thick white gauze ended at the middle of my thigh…and then nothing.

In the back of my mind, I could hear Knox explaining how he did everything he could to save it, but there was just too much damage. I started tuning him out as he went deep into the medical terminology and discussions of physical therapy.

My mind wandered back to the mountainside. I could still taste the cordite and smoke in the air, still feel my pounding heart as the bomber's loud roar drew closer and closer. A sharp pain erupted near my kneecap, and I flew head first into the ground. I could recall the excruciating pain I felt, and the fear as Emersyn ran toward me.

A part of me knew she wasn't going to reach me in time, and I knew I didn't want her to. I remembered getting to my feet and forcing myself to keep running and then a wall of fire throwing me into the air.

Leaning back, images of a pool of blood surrounding my leg flashed behind my eyes. Emersyn's pale face and round eyes shouting for Doc, even though her skin bubbled from the wall of heat she ran into

A shallow breath escaped my lips as I continued to stare at the mattress where my leg should have been. Anger surged through me, and I snapped my head up to Knox's gaze.

"How long were you planning to wait?" I waved a hand toward my leg. "It's not like I wouldn't have noticed something was missing."

He opened his mouth, but I turned my head away from him, refusing to hear any excuses. I shook my head and huffed. "Unbelievable."

As quickly as my anger had come, it transformed into grief. Tears pooled in my eyes. Refusing to meet anyone's gazes, I stared forward and bit down hard on the inside of my cheek.

You will not cry...you will not cry. Not in front of everyone.

"Greer," Mom whispered.

I swallowed back the emotion swirling inside of me. "I'm really tired," I stated tonelessly.

From the corner of my eye, I saw Knox nod. He injected a

needle into my IV line. "This will help you sleep and keep away any discomfort you feel."

I didn't comment. I kept my face forward as the warm sensation drifted through my body. The darkness came swooping in, and this time I welcomed it.

Chapter 27

THE NEXT DAY, WHEN PEOPLE CAME TO VISIT ME, I pretended to sleep. Even when my sisters stopped by, I kept my eyes closed.

I didn't want to see anyone.

I didn't know what to say.

I didn't know how to act.

All I wanted was time to myself so I could process everything.

Amerie came to my room several times, and each time Mom gently told her I hadn't woken up yet. Toward the end of the day, I heard Mom walk out the door with her so they could talk in the hallway.

I didn't care to listen. A part of me knew I was acting like a petulant child, but the other part didn't care.

The sun began its slow descent into the sky when my parents finally gave in for the day. I felt their arms wrap around me in a tight embrace.

"We'll be back in the morning, Kid," Dad whispered.

"Get some rest," Mom added.

I waited several heartbeats after my door closed behind them. When I thought it was safe, I just barely opened one eye. Seeing nothing, I leaned my head back and sighed as I opened my eyes for the first time today.

I pulled back the blanket and just stared at what was left

of my leg. Lightly, I ran my fingers over the bandaged stump. Tears filled my eyes, and I let them fall freely down my face.

All of the feelings I had bottled up came pouring out.

How was I ever going to ride again?

Play with Beth?

I couldn't fight for my country anymore.

I had always wanted to open my gym someday; how could I do that now?

The endless questions kept flying through my mind, tormenting me. Quiet sobs wracked my body, and I cradled my arms tightly against my chest. The tears began to slow, and I took a shaky breath. Wiping my eyes, I felt some of the weight lift off my chest.

I leaned my head against my pillow as exhaustion pulled my eyelids down.

FOOTSTEPS PIERCED through my sleep-hazed mind. They marched with a purpose around my bed to the side of my room. A snapping sound filled my ears, and then a blast of sunlight blared down on me in full force.

I scrunched up my face and twisted away from the offending light.

"It's time to wake up, Greer Martha."

I looked up to see Dad staring down at me. "You had all day yesterday to feel sorry for yourself. You're not doing that today."

Groaning, I turned my head to the side and saw Mom wearing an expectant expression.

"What do you do when a horse bucks you off?"

"Get back on," I answered immediately.

Mom nodded. "Are you going to get back on, or are you going to stay on the ground, beaten?"

My mouth parted as her words hit me. Shame cascaded through me. I was a SEAL. SEALs didn't give up. We fought.

Nodding, I felt my spark slowly reignite within my bones. "Yes, ma'am." I met her gaze and frowned slightly. "Do you think I'll still be able to ride?"

"You're still breathing, ain't ya?" Dad asked.

My lips curved up as a small chuckle escaped. "Yes, sir."

He nodded. "Nothing has ever stopped you before. This won't either."

Hearing the unwavering confidence in his tone caused a lump to form in my throat. I nodded and swallowed.

I wanted to tell them they had done everything for me. Turned me into someone I could be proud of. Gave me the strength to always fight, that I wouldn't be anything without them, but instead, only a simple thank you came out.

From the glossy glint in their eyes, I knew they understood.

Mom wiped away a tear and smiled down at me. "Someone is here to see you. I called her after you woke up. She's traveled a long way to visit with you."

I felt my eyebrows pull together. "Who—"

A petite woman with grey hair walked into my room. The air rushed from my lungs as a pair of green eyes met mine.

Mom squeezed my hand. "I'll let you and Ms. Ann catch up."

I watched my parents slip from the room before meeting Angelette's mom's eyes again. She waved toward the chair by my bed. "May I?"

I nodded. "Yes, ma'am." I grabbed the bed remote and raised the top half until I was in a sitting position.

Ms. Ann looked over my body before meeting my gaze

again. "I want to apologize for how I acted the last time we met."

I shook my head. "You were right." The lump came back. "It was my job to protect your daughter, and I failed."

Ms. Ann held up her hand halting me. "I know you and your team did everything you could to save my Angelette. I knew it then, but I was hurt and angry, and you were an easy target for me to blame."

I looked down at the blanket and sighed. "She never should have been there."

Ms. Ann laughed, drawing my gaze back to her. "You couldn't have talked Angelette into leaving her friends behind."

I felt the corners of my own mouth twitch. "I could have tried."

She smiled. "It wouldn't have done any good."

Probably not.

Images of Angelette's smiling face flashed through my mind. I traced the winged piercing.

Ms. Ann reached into her bag and pulled out a worn leather journal. I gasped as I recognized it as the journal Angelette always had with her.

Ms. Ann's fingers caressed the worn leather. "This was sent to my house a few days after we met." Her green eyes glistened with unshed tears. "Reading this really helped me, and I think it will help you too."

I began to shake my head as she placed the journal on top of my fingers. "I can't take this from you."

"I have a room filled with Angelette's work. Besides," she smiled warmly at me, "I think you could use this more than me."

I grasped the worn leather. Not sure what to say, I stared at the journal until a warm hand squeezed mine.

"You have a challenging road ahead of you, but I know you can overcome it. You are one of the bravest individuals I have ever met." She released my hand and smiled. "It takes courage to never quit fighting."

My throat clogged with emotion. "Thank you."

She nodded as she wiped away a fallen tear. "You and your sisters don't be strangers, okay?"

This time I grabbed her hand. "Of course not." I chuckled softly. "You've already been adopted into this dysfunctional family."

She laughed. "I'm honored." Smiling, she stood up. "I hope the journal helps you find some peace." She bent down and wrapped me in a gentle hug. "I can see why Angelette spoke so fondly of you all."

Ignoring the choking lump, I met her gaze. "Your daughter was a great friend. She inspires me to be a better person every day."

Ms. Ann swiped away a few tears. She looked down at her watch and smiled. "I'd better go. Amerie invited me to a poker tournament they're having in the cafeteria."

Oh boy...

"Don't trust her," I warned. "She's a card shark."

Laughter so similar to Angelette's filled my small room. "I am well aware." Still chuckling, she walked out the door.

Smiling, I turned my attention back to leather journal in my lap. I took a deep breath and slowly opened it. The pages fluttered down to a leather strap holding a page halfway through the journal. The title, *Eternal Flame*, was inked at the top of the page. Taking another deep breath, I began to read.

Give me strength, for I am weak.
My struggles are demanding me to be meek.

Once again, I have been knocked down to my knees.
Beaten and battered blue, my fire no longer burns with ease.
Negative, shouting voices fill my head.
They push on my body and weigh me down with lead.
The breath I release comes out in a weary pant.
I know the easy way out is something life will not give away
nor grant.
Stranded, I desperately latch onto the small flame that burns
within me.
Its warmth rekindles my fighting soul, allowing me to
properly see.
Peace fills my mind, making me realize I'll never be given
more than I can handle.
Heat spreads throughout my body as I refuse to be blown out
like a candle.
Bruised but not broken, I slowly rise to my feet.
Ignited with determination, I will not bow down or accept
defeat.

FOR SEVERAL SECONDS, I forgot how to breathe. I read the poem again, and then once more before setting the journal down. A small smile began to spread across my lips.

I looked up toward the ceiling. "Thank you, Angelette."

The words she had written seemed to speak directly to me. I could feel the fire that burned within each line. A renewed strength coursed through my muscles.

My flame will never flicker out.

Next to my bed, a wheelchair stood within grabbing distance. Reaching out, I pulled the chair close and set the brakes. I scooted my body to the edge of the bed.

My muscles ached in protest as sweat began to dot across

my forehead. Inhaling deeply, I used one hand to push my body off the bed while the other hand gripped the chair handle tightly.

Pain radiated from my ribcage and lower right side of my body, but I ignored it as I plopped down into the seat. My breath came out in ragged pants. Letting some of the pain die down, I sat in the chair and took several deep breaths.

Once the pain became more manageable, I slowly wheeled myself around the bed and out the door. My smile and confidence grew the farther down the hall I traveled. I had just reached the end of the hallway when Knox rounded the corner.

He skidded to a stop and gaped at me.

"Greer…" His mouth dropped as he looked at the wheel-chair, to my room, and then back to me. "You are supposed to be in bed, you need rest."

I wanted to roll my eyes, but I resisted the urge.

I was done resting.

"I'm ready to start working, and getting back on my feet."

Still staring with wide eyes, Knox slowly shook his head. "You shouldn't have been able to transfer yourself to that chair."

Leaning back, I held his gaze as my lips curved up into a devilish smirk. "When are you going to learn?" My eyes danced with mischief as I arched an eyebrow at him. "Never underestimate a woman."

Epilogue
one year later

SUNLIGHT WARMED THE BACK OF MY SKIN AS WE WALKED through the iron gates. Flowers bloomed around the walkway and bright green leaves filled the surrounding trees.

Breathing in the smell of freshly mowed grass, a small smile popped onto my face. I loved the springtime.

I looked down at my legs. One had the beginning of a tan starting to show while the other stood out in an eye-popping turquoise. My prosthetic leg, created by the latest 3-D technology, had become my favorite feature on my body.

It reminded me every day I was a fighter. A survivor.

I twisted my head to the side and smiled at the queen Punisher "tattoo" just above where my ankle should have been.

Amerie had insisted I get the symbol during one of our many physical therapy sessions. After an exceptionally brutal session, I finally gave in to her pleas and went with her and the rest of my sisters to get it done. Now, I couldn't imagine going anywhere without my signature ink.

My gaze wandered down to Amerie's ankle where her skin sported the same black tat. She walked with a slight limp, but it didn't slow her down, especially in the water.

Her smile spread from ear to ear as she walked down the road. "So, Sheba, I've been thinking about your bachelorette party…"

Dee arched an eyebrow at her. "That kind of scares me."

Emersyn snickered while Amerie just shrugged. "Don't be like that." Amerie gave Dee a pointed stare, but her lips never wavered. "Granny and I were thinking Vegas since you live in New Orleans." Amerie made a face. "Well, actually, Vegas was technically Joker and Hollywood's idea, but Granny and I planned everything."

Dee stopped and stared at Amerie. "I wasn't aware Granny and the boys were coming for the bachelorette party."

Amerie gaped at her. "She's your maid of honor...of course she's coming. And how could we leave the boys out of this? They're you're brides-men."

Emersyn shook her head, chuckling. "We might actually become rich with Legacy and Granny at the tables."

I smirked. "Or dirt poor."

Amerie rolled her eyes at me. "Just because we know how to win and you don't, doesn't mean we need to hear your negativity." She nudged me with her shoulder. "You and Knoxy will probably be the next ones getting hitched."

Chuckling, I held up my hands. "Slow down. We've only been dating for a few months."

Amerie smirked. "I'm calling it now."

Following the curve of the road, I shook my head at her. We stepped off the gravel road and walked across the grass until we stopped in front of a tall pair of angel wings.

Emersyn bent down and placed a bouquet of flowers just below Angelette's smiling face.

"We have a surprise for you, Angelette." Emersyn looked back at all of us with a huge grin.

I nodded at her. "You do the honors."

Emersyn glanced back at Angelette. "You're going to be a published author. Tomorrow is the big release day."

Just as Ms. Ann had said, Angelette's journal had helped me find peace as well as my fire. On some of my toughest days after leaving the hospital in Germany, I'd relied on Angelette to get me through it all.

After each of us had read the journal, we all knew we had to get it published. Thanks to Emersyn and Ms. Ann, it was now becoming a reality.

Dee patted the wings. "You'd be proud of how everything turned out."

Amerie nodded. "Yeah, Americans finally got their shit together and are actually getting along and working with one another." She cut a side glance toward me and wriggled her eyebrows. "The snowflakes have melted."

I shook my head at her, and she shrugged. "What?"

Instead of answering, I turned back toward Angelette. "We've got tighter sanctions than ever in both North Korea and Russia, and the radical jihadists have been kicked down into submission."

Amerie smirked at my description. "I'm not sure if we'll ever fully stop their ideology, but they know better than attacking on American soil." Amerie pushed her fingers together and made an explosion sound with her mouth.

Dee chuckled. "I'd think twice too. Those Big Mother bombs are no joke."

After the official surrender from both Russia and North Korea, ISIS attempted an attack in Washington. That didn't go over so well with the president. He ordered an immediate attack on Syria, targeting a massive stronghold of ISIS rebels with a new weapon appropriately named Big Mother.

Needless to say, terrorist attacks had ceased.

At least for the time being anyway. I had a feeling ISIS or some other radicalized group would try something again, but I knew this time, America would be ready to fight fire with fire.

Amerie patted the stone. "And we're all doing good.

Sheba's getting married in two months." She winked at Dee. "We're going to Vegas to celebrate properly."

Dee and I shared looks.

"You know you can't stop her," I mouthed.

Dee rolled her eyes, but the smile on her face gave away her true feelings.

"Bookie is crazy as ever. Training for her next marathon, and eventually the Olympics." Amerie twirled her finger around beside her head and mouthed, "Loco," at Emersyn before continuing. "I'm officially a Texan, and with my business partner, Kid, we'll be opening our gym, Queen Bs." She smiled at me and then wrapped an arm around the stone wings. "And last but not least, we are all co-founders, with your mom, of the non-profit organization Angel Wings, which helps veterans cope with the struggles of war after coming home."

I nodded. "Your mom has been amazing."

We stood in front of the statue, each lost in our own thoughts. Blue flashed by, and I turned my head slightly to see a blue jay perched on a branch. My lips curved up.

I watched the bird hop from branch to branch before it raised its wings and soared off toward the sun. Emersyn smiled as she glimpsed the bird's departure. She walked over and wrapped her arms around mine and Dee's waists. Reaching over, I wrapped my other arm around Amerie.

Together, we stood around Angelette.

One big, happy, dysfunctional family.

I couldn't imagine my life without these brave and courageous women. We had seen and done more together in a short period of time than what most people did in a lifetime. It made me excited for our future adventures together.

Smiling, I tightened my hold on my sisters. "Here's to new beginnings."

Sneak Peak

Honor
Angelette's Story

All the great things are simple, and many can be expressed in a single word: freedom, justice, honor, duty, mercy, hope.

- Winston Churchill

Entry 1

Mom, I wish I could say the words to make you understand, but you and I both know I've always been better at writing my thoughts than actually expressing them.

So many times I started to tell you the truth, but then, for some reason or another, I'd find some excuse to postpone the inevitable.

Now, I'm flying out of the country and I have run out of time.

As I travel farther away from home, the guilt of my betrayal weighs heavily on my chest. I believed my silence protected you from unnecessary worry, but now I realize I lied to myself and to you.

Admiral Grace Murray Hopper said it best, "It's easier to ask for forgiveness than to ask permission."

As you read my truth, I hope you can find a way to forgive me.

Acknowledgments

This amazing journey that has allowed me to bring the Sister-hood Series to life has been an experience I will cherish my entire life. I am grateful beyond words to everyone who has made this all possible.

Thank you to my family and friends. Your love and never-ending support are what push me to keep going. I love each and every one of you.

Mom, Gillian, and Dennis, you all deserve a huge round of applauds for finding all of my errors and Chelsi-isms. *Courage* would not have turned out the way it did without y'all's sharp eyes. I appreciate all that you have done!

To Bienvenue Press, I cannot say thank you enough for making all of this possible. I and the sisterhood are honored and humbled you chose to work with us. Thank you.

About the Author

Chelsi Arnold was born and raised in Texas, (And yes, like most Texans she tends to be a little biased to the fact that everything is bigger and better in Texas) – but hey, it ain't bragging if it's true ;) Chelsi grew up in a single-stop-light town where she spent most of her time playing sports and going to rodeos. Throughout Chelsi's life, her goals and dreams have changed, but having a close relationship with her friends and family, and her love for creativity has always remained. Chelsi is a firm believer that anything is possible, as long as you work hard and have determination; there is nothing you cannot accomplish.

 facebook.com/ChelsiAnneleArnold

twitter.com/ChelsiArnold

"'Embrace The Suck' is the theme of this unbelievable story.
God, I don't even know where to begin with this review
because I had such a guttural reaction while reading it.
BRAVE is the first book in the new "Sisterhood Series". Back
in the 80's I read Stephen King's THE STAND which was
written pre-AIDS. As I was reading it, I thought he must have
known something while writing it because the plague he
wrote about was so much like the epidemic that was
spreading while I was reading it. Well I got the same feeling
reading BRAVE!" —Amazon Review

Don't miss Book One in the Sisterhood Series!
Amazon Buy Link: http://a.co/d/0xTUBBd

BIENVENUE PRESS

Be the first to hear about other new books from Bienvenue Press!

Sign up for announcements about new releases, and sales at

http://eepurl.com/dnC-jH!

Follow us on social media:
Twitter: https://twitter.com/BienvenuePress
Facebook: https://www.facebook.com/bienvenuepress/
Bienvenue Press Readers and Writers Group:
https://www.facebook.com/groups/1752871518355266
Instagram: https://www.instagram.com/bienvenuepress/